The Last Vanguard

Book One of the Sevordine Chronicles

by
Shawn P. B. Robinson

BrainSwell Publishing
Ingersoll, Ontario

Copyright © 2023 Shawn P. B. Robinson

All rights reserved. The use of any part of this publication reproduced, transmitted in any form or by any means, electronic, mechanical, photocopying, recording, or otherwise, or stored in a retrieval system, without the prior written consent of the publisher is an infringement of the copyright law.

ISBN 978-1-989296-44-8

Cover design and artwork copyright © Shawn Robinson
Interior Page Dividers designed from images downloaded from Freepick.com.

BrainSwell Publishing
Ingersoll, ON

Dedication and Thanks

To Ezra, who loves this story.
To Juanita for so much awesome feedback.
To Liam, who is always so supportive.
To all of you, cause you're awesome!

This book is a work of fiction.
Characters and places and such are fictional. I mean… there are trolls in here! How often do you see trolls in real life? I… wait… okay… bad example. Switching gears… There are Shaloomd in here! When have you seen a Shaloomd flying around above your head? I mean, seriously? This book is fiction. How can you not know that?

Preface

The idea for this story hit me while I was trying to take a nap. I lay back in a chair in our living room, trying to fall asleep, when the story idea hit me, and I spent my entire precious nap time working through the story.

Now, I'm happy that the story came to me, but I'm still a little resentful to the story for costing me my nap. You can't get those things back!

Shawn P. B. Robinson

CHECK OUT THESE BOOKS BY
Shawn P. B. Robinson

Adult Fiction (Sci-fi & Fantasy)

The Ridge Series (3 books)
ADA: An Anthology of Short Stories

YA Fiction (Fantasy)

The Sevordine Chronicles (5 Books)

Books for Younger Readers

Annalynn the Canadian Spy Series (6 Books)
Jerry the Squirrel (4 Books)
Arestana Series (3 Books)
Activity Books (2 Books)

www.shawnpbrobinson.com/books

Table of Contents

1

The Castle

Pain explodes in my face, and my head jerks off to the side. Flashes of light and strange colors fill my vision. I feel like the world has begun to spin, and I don't even realize that I'm heading toward the ground until my cheek slams against the hard dirt.

I take a moment and try to regain my senses. I shake my head, but it only hurts, and I quickly stop. Behind me, Rulf is screaming something unintelligible. I don't know if it doesn't make sense because it's Rulf or because I just took a fist to the head.

I push myself up slowly, hoping Rulf will get bored and move on. He sounds angry, though. When he gets mad, there's only one person who can stop him.

Once on my feet, I turn around and face the boy… or man. I'm not sure what he is. He's tall enough that he towers over me, and I'm taller than most. I think he's younger than me, too, but while I'm barely shaving, he has a dark shadow that suggests a decent beard is only about two days away.

"I'm sorry, Rulf. I made a mistake," I say loudly. I once tried speaking quietly to him, and he punched me to teach me a lesson. "I'm just out to buy some salt."

"Do you have money?" Rulf growls.

I let out a sigh, careful not to let Rulf see. Reaching into my pocket, I grab the money I was given. I don't have to worry about Rulf robbing me. Rulf is not a thief. Well, he's a bit of a thief. He steals food from people for him and Mic, but I could drop a hundred golds at his feet, and he'd never touch it. Even if he wanted to, Mic wouldn't let him.

I hold out my hand, and Rulf checks the four silvers. He takes his time counting them, but I know it's a show. He pretends to be dumb, but he's anything but that. He's only checking to make sure I'm telling him the truth. He hates it when people lie to him—especially us "castle brats".

He nods, and I take that as permission to put the coins back in my pocket. Taking a small step back, he brings himself to his full height. It's hard to believe how tall he is. He's not built as large as the men who work in the mines and certainly nothing like a blacksmith, but he's quite solid. They say he has giant blood in him. If that's the case, he probably still has a lot of growing to do. When he gets bigger, I don't ever want to run into him.

I turn to leave, but Rulf grabs me with one hand, lifts me off my feet, and shouts, "Did I tell you that you could walk away?"

He raises his fist to hit me again. There's nothing I can do. I saw a man try to hold him down once. Rulf picked him up and nearly threw him onto a second-floor balcony. With that kind of inhuman strength, even the soldiers give Rulf his space.

I'd rather not lose any teeth, so I close my eyes, turn my head, and prepare for what's coming. I'm kind of hoping that I'll black out, and Rulf will get bored.

Quick footsteps approach. "Don't hurt much! Don't hurt much!"

I relax. Mic has arrived. I might get out of here without any more bruises. Mic is the only one who can stop the big guy.

Rulf lets go, and I drop to the ground. When I open my eyes, I see Rulf has turned and is grunting at Mic. Mic is a little shorter than I am, has terribly messy hair all the time and usually has a large bruise on his face. They say that Rulf beats Mic when he can't find anyone else, but I don't believe it. Rulf cares for Mic like he's a younger brother.

Mic steps up next to me and clumsily pulls me to my feet as he mumbles, "Sorry, you. Sorry, you."

His eyes dart all over the place, and his shoulders jerk back and forth in Mic's typical style. A bit of drool hangs from the side of his mouth, and it appears as though part of his lunch is still on his chin.

"Go, you. Go, you." Mic says, his eyes following some imaginary point as it moves past his face. He gives me a light push, then turns back to Rulf. He waves at his huge friend and says, "Eat. Eat," before wandering off with Rulf a short distance behind.

I pull up my shirt and check my side. The first hit landed just on my ribs. I know Rulf would have no trouble breaking any of my bones, but he didn't. That tells me the big guy is holding back somewhat. There is that, at least. A large, swollen, red area identifies where my bruise will form, if I didn't already have the pain to let me know. I'm sure my face will look pretty nasty by tomorrow.

With this setback, I now need to rush. Tereese needs the salt right away. Can't remember what for, but it doesn't matter. If she sends me for salt and tells me to get it back to her right away… I just go.

I run north toward the market, weaving in and out among the people. If I'd known Rulf was on that street, I'd have taken a different route. I normally avoid him when I'm out, but today he just stepped out of an alley, and I ran right into him. He's not the forgiving type.

I turn left, then right, and a few minutes later, I'm at the market. I find Old Sweaty and tell him I need a sack of salt. The poor guy's name is Set or Smet or something, but it had become Old Sweaty at one point. He isn't even all that old. I'd ask him what his actual name is, but I've known him my whole life. I can't just ask him at this point without revealing that I don't know something as basic as his name.

I pay Old Sweaty and take my sack of salt, then turn and run. Tereese won't be pleased. When she wants something from the market, every second counts.

I hear Rulf yelling at someone at one point along the way, but Mic is there calming him down. The two are close, and I rarely see them apart. It's a good thing, too. Without Mic, I fear no one would be safe. I expect the soldiers would try to arrest Rulf if Mic weren't there to calm him down, but I'm not sure they could manage it. If they tried to kill him… well… if he really has giant blood, can they even kill someone like that?

I like Mic, though. Everyone does, but he stays out of sight. He won't look anyone in the eye and is hardly recognizable from day to day with the bruises and the dirt on his face. But Rulf takes pretty good care of the kid.

When I reach the castle, I just run past the guards. They barely look at me—just another servant in the castle. Some of the soldiers like me. Some don't. The biggest one I have to avoid is Captain Tilbur. The guy despises me, but as long as I keep my distance, he never seeks me out.

I head straight for the kitchens, but I'm not even in the door when I hear her.

"Caric!" Tereese yells. "What took you so long? My soup is just about ready!" She stops when she gets close and

4

examines my face. With a deep frown, she asks, "Did you pick a fight with Rulf again?"

"No, Ma'am." Tereese is never one to correct. If she thinks I'm the one that picks the fights, there's no benefit to telling her I'm not.

She shakes her head and takes the bag of salt from me. Without another word, she turns away and hollers out to one of her assistants, letting him know the salt has arrived.

I turn around and nearly run over Marleet. Her slight frame and lack of height make her easy to overlook at times.

Marleet doesn't ask for permission as she gently runs her fingers across the area on my face where Rulf struck me. She seems to be deep in thought, trying to figure it all out. Marleet is one of the sweetest, kindest, prettiest girls I have ever met. She's always concerned for other people and genuinely excited about everything that's important to them. Unfortunately, she takes her time working through matters.

"I think, Caric," she says to me with a look of concentration on her face, "that someone might have punched you again."

I nod my head slowly. It sounds like she felt I needed to be informed of that fact. I'm not sure what else I need to say.

"Wait here." She smiles sweetly and rushes off. As she goes, her beautiful dress, which is far too formal for working in the kitchen, flows behind her. She always dresses in the prettiest outfit she can find at every opportunity.

I know she's trying to catch the eye of Hemot, but the guy seems oblivious to it. He's asked out just about every girl within a few years of his age, except the one girl who can't keep her eyes off him. I'm beginning to think it's because Hemot feels he'd have no chance with a girl like Marleet. The two of them are so weird.

Marleet returns a moment later with a cloth. Inside is a piece of ice she's chipped off a block in the icehouse. I grab the cloth from her and hide it under my shirt before Tereese can see. If the head cook of the castle sees Marleet take ice without asking... well... Marleet will get in trouble.

I smile and thank her before I move on. Once out of the kitchen area, I put the ice on my face and rush into the castle. Now that my errand is finished, I need to get back to Ellcia. She won't be happy about having to clean the third-floor corridor all by herself.

As I enter the hallway, I stop for a moment. I realize I have many people in my life who get angry with me. I don't really like that, but what do you do about that kind of thing?

When I find Ellcia, she's humming softly to herself, but jumps when I approach. I hate scaring her, but it's nearly impossible not to. When she sets her mind to work and starts humming, she forgets about everything else, and it's just a matter of time before I scare her.

"Rulf again?" she asks.

"Yup."

"What happened this time?"

"I bumped into him," I say, rolling my eyes. "I was trying to be so careful, but he just stepped out of an alley, and before I knew it, my shoulder had touched him."

"Where did you get the ice? Marleet?" she asks me with a smile.

"Yup."

She stands and wanders over to me, pretending she's wearing a large, beautiful dress instead of the plain red trousers given to the cleaning staff. When she reaches me, she runs her hands gently over my face. I focus so as not to blush. I didn't mind Marleet checking my bruise. I absolutely adore Marleet and love spending time with her, but I only ever want a friendship with her.

Ellcia, on the other hand...

Ellcia says to me in a perfect impersonation of Marleet, "I think, Caric, that you might have been punched."

She laughs, and our eyes meet for a moment before I look away.

"That's pretty close to what happened."

"It was nice of her to get you the ice," she says with another smile, but before I can respond, she says, "But... you have missed a lot of the work. I've cleaned most of the corridor already. We need to wipe down the statues, the busts, the armor, and the windowsills. Hemot should be here to take care of the curtains before long. Let's get to work. We need to at least start on the General's Ballroom this afternoon."

I nod and dive in, holding the ice to my face with my left hand while I work on wiping down the sills. I'll get to the two-handed jobs in a bit once the ice is mostly gone.

About an hour later, Ellcia and I are chatting about the latest news we've heard from the Talic Region when two soldiers enter the corridor. That, in itself, is not unusual, but these two men have red sashes across their chests and walk with their hands on their swords. I immediately step to the side of the room next to Ellcia. We stand straight, but with our heads bowed.

A moment later, the Regent himself enters the corridor, walking right by Ellcia without a word. It's not that he doesn't like her. He just doesn't seem to notice that she exists.

"Ah, Caric," he says to me, and I step forward obediently. "Raise your head."

I do, and we meet eyes. He's a little shorter than me, but I'm thin. The Regent, because of a lifestyle of meetings and feasts, is quite my opposite in that regard. As soon as I raise my face, his eyes drift to my cheek. I gather that means the ice didn't solve the problem.

He laughs. "You were in a fight again, weren't you, Caric?" Behind the Regent stands Captain Tilbur, his height and build making the rest of us look tiny. When the Regent takes a glance at the Captain, the man scowls at me.

I give a quick bow. "Yes, Regent."

"Well, I guess that's normal for young men of your position. I was never one to get in a fight when I was younger, but I'm royalty, of course."

"Yes, Regent."

He laughs again and turns to Captain Tilbur. "It's probably for the best. Maybe it's a good way for the young man to get some exercise."

Tilbur smiles at me with nothing but malice in his eyes. "Yes, running is wonderful exercise. I expect the child gets many such opportunities to stretch his legs. If he continues to run like this, he might one day compete in the games."

I don't mind Tilbur's comments about running, but the comment about being a child bothers me. I'm almost an adult, but it doesn't actually matter how old I am. I'm just a servant. I've heard men four times my age referred to as children. It's the way of things for those of us who serve.

"But it'll help to make him strong," the Regent says. He puts a hand on my shoulder and says in a quiet and serious voice, "You know, Caric, I have told you this before, but I am grateful every day that you are with us. I never thought I'd be able to rescue you and your friends."

"Thank you, Regent," I say with a small bow. "I have never forgotten what you did for us."

The Regent then, in an uncharacteristic move, turns to Ellcia as if noticing her for the first time. He tells her to raise her head, and he examines her for a moment. I feel nervous for Ellcia, and Tilbur looks angry. I'm not sure if Ellcia and I will suffer for this later on. When Tilbur frowns, I worry. We'll need to avoid the Captain for the next few days.

"And this one," the Regent says. "She looks familiar to me. Has she been with us for a while?"

Tilbur shifts on his feet. "Yes, Regent Parthun. She was one of the children you rescued, along with the boy."

The Regent continues in the same tone, not addressing Ellcia, but speaking to Tilbur. "She's turning out to be quite the pretty one, don't you think, Captain? Perhaps not as pretty as the blond one down in the kitchens, but pretty enough. Maybe we'll need to appoint her to work as a serving girl in the banquet hall."

"Perhaps." The Captain grinds his teeth, and his cheeks flush. Whatever we've done to upset him this time, it's not going to be fun when we have to face him later. "But," he says in a near growl, "we need to move on. The General is waiting to speak with you."

"Right!" the Regent says and turns back to me. "Have a wonderful day, Caric." He reaches up and pats me on my cheek, right where Rulf hit me. I do my best not to wince. "Make sure you do your work well and to the best of your ability."

Once the Regent and Captain, along with their guard, have moved on, I turn to Ellcia. She has an uncomfortable look on her face.

"That's the first time he's spoken to me. Well, he didn't actually speak to me. He just asked the Captain about me."

I don't know how to respond to that, so I remain silent. Everyone tells me I'm the Regent's favorite servant. I can't imagine that he has a favorite servant, but it's hard to deny that he treats me differently than the rest.

We get back to work, and I start on the statues. I always hate cleaning them. I climb up and do my best to get to every area, but the rough stone collects dust, and the cloths catch on everything.

But all the work comes to a halt a few minutes later when Hemot races up. He has a wild look in his eyes, and his grin stretches across his face. "Caric! Ellcia! Come quick! The Regent is talking about the Prince!"

2

---●---

The Idea

Hemot races down the hall, and I keep close on his heels. Ellcia runs right behind me. She's not an overly fast runner, and I don't want to leave her behind. My heart is pounding, but not from the running. I'm actually in pretty great shape. The Captain is right about one thing, I do get a lot of exercise because of Rulf.

Everyone gets excited when the topic of the Prince comes up. No one knows where he might be, but everyone's sure he's still alive. It's been about eleven years since Lord Parthun, now Regent Parthun, swept in and put an end to the Revolt. He'd only arrived a few hours too late. In that time, not only were the King and Queen killed, but my parents along with Ellcia's, Hemot's, Marleet's, and many others all met their end. They say the Prince fled into the Talic Region and lives in one of the cities, or in the countryside, or in the mountains, or by the sea, or any number of places, depending on the rumor and who tells it.

On the way, Hemot explains as best as he can while we run. "General Corter and Captain Tilbur are meeting with the Regent." He speaks quietly while we race down the halls. "The people keep demanding that he send out more search parties for the Prince. They say since he should be nearly seventeen by now, he must be found and placed on the throne."

"Do they have any new rumors on where he might be?" I ask. I notice the other two are nearly gasping for air by this point, but I'm breathing fairly well. I guess there have been a lot of errands for salt.

"Not really," Hemot says. "Just more about him in the Talic Region."

We turn a corner and nearly run into Marleet. Her face fills with shock until she sees Hemot. "Hi," she begins, but then Hemot grabs her arm and drags her along. I can see she's flustered at first, but then her face fills with excitement. Unaware of what's going on, she does her best to run alongside Hemot.

We reach the area near the throne room, and Hemot slows right down. The four of us walk calmly in single file with our hands behind our backs, as is fitting in such an area of the castle. We make our way past the same two guards I saw in the corridor with the Regent as they stand at the two large ornately carved doors leading into the throne room where the Regent rules in place of the King.

With how excited we are, it's hard to keep our speed down, but Hemot leads us along the corridor and then takes us to the left, out of sight of the guards. I look up and down the corridor to confirm that no one is in sight, while Hemot slips his fingers into a small hole in the wall and pulls. The wall gives way and opens to a small area, and the four of us slip inside and pull the wall closed behind us. I smile at Hemot and nod my head. He's just recently oiled the hinges, and it was a good idea.

There's only one tiny hole leading into the throne room, so none of us can peer through without blocking the sound from the others. When we first found the small secret room, Ellcia had insisted we report it. It was, after all, a serious security issue, but Hemot and I refused. There are no actual threats to the kingdom at the moment. Everyone's at peace. There are no wars. The people love the Regent and trust him to rule well as he has for eleven years. Poverty is all but abolished, and trade is booming.

No one would want to spy. Even if they did, they wouldn't know about the room. Hemot had only found the place because he had been bored and chanced upon it while pretending to work.

Each of us lean in as close as we can to the hole. Marleet's managed to place herself right next to Hemot in the small area, and we all concentrate on what we hear.

"There are always rumors!" an irritated voice says. I easily recognize it as the Regent's. He sounds frustrated. "What's different about these ones?"

"Nothing," the General's voice booms out. He's one of those people whose voice carries across rooms or large areas. I've often thought that it was probably part of what makes him a good General.

"You?" the Regent asks.

I recognize the next voice as Captain Tilbur's. "Well, the newest rumors seem to be a little more intense. They aren't that much different from the rest, but there are a lot of rumors now, and new ones are coming constantly. Whether there's any truth to any of them or not, people *believe* there's truth to them."

Tilbur's not as loud as General Corter, but he's… dangerous. Everyone knows General Corter leads the army, but every soldier fears Captain Tilbur. Tilbur also has the advantage of being huge. He's big, nearly bald, and looks like he wants to kill someone. But, it wouldn't matter how big he is. He is a dangerous man. People only cross him once.

Between those two men, it's clear who's really in charge.

"And what do these rumors say about him?" the Regent asks. The irritation is still in his voice, but it doesn't sound like it's directed at the Captain.

Tilbur answers, "Mostly the same as always. He's been seen here or there, or someone's cousin knows a guy who spoke with him or things like that. But they all involve seeing him in the Talic Region. What's interesting, though, is that most of these rumors center on him being in one of the two northern cities."

There's silence for a few moments, and my heart begins to beat quickly. I'm not sure if the meeting is suddenly over, but we need to get out of here before we're caught. It seems like an odd way to end a meeting.

I nearly breathe a sigh of relief when the Regent says, "Morgin and Haner?" referring to two of the big cities in that region. The other two cities, Leito and Rainer, are farther south.

"Yes, Regent," the Captain replies.

"Just because people are pointing to specific cities, doesn't mean there's anything to this!" the General hollers out. "Tilbur, do you really think we should waste soldiers on a fruitless search?"

"Not at all!" Tilbur replies, and he sounds like a smile has broken out on his face. "I think the people are quite worked up about this whole situation. I suspect the people would appreciate some effort at this point in time."

"The Prince is not in the Talic Region," the Regent says.

I'm surprised to hear that. I had thought the Regent didn't know where the Prince was. It leaves me quite confused, but I push that thought down.

"Regent," the Captain says, "not one of us believes the Prince is out there. I would agree that if he's still alive, he's likely closer to home. However, there is a chance that he's in the Talic Region. If so, I would think it would be best to identify where he is. If not, well… honestly, how many of the search parties do you think will make it back?"

I think I hear someone laugh, but I'm sure it must just be my imagination. The Regent is probably reacting to the fear that the search parties might be in danger. He's a good man.

There's silence for a long time. After a bit, Hemot leans forward and peers through the hole for a second. He pulls back and signals to us that things are okay. We wait until the conversation starts up again.

"Yes," the Regent says. "I think I will send out search parties."

"Is this for the best?" General Corter asks.

In a caring and compassionate voice, the Regent replies, "If there's a chance, we must try."

Loud laughter erupts from the room, and I look over at my friends. All of them are as confused as I am. I don't know what's supposed to be so funny.

"Captain," the Regent says, "see to it. Organize the search parties. Allow people to volunteer for it and give them their traveling papers. I would like a minimum of four parties sent out, one to each of the major cities." There's a slight pause before he adds, "Call them the Vanguards."

I smile to myself. I think that's a really great name, and I hope that means there will be more search parties in the future. Maybe they'll continue until we find our missing Prince.

"Yes, Regent," Captain Tilbur replies. "But won't the name suggest we'll be sending more search parties in the future?"

"It will pacify the people for now, and then, if the Vanguard fails, then we'll tell the people we won't risk any more lives," Regent Parthun declares.

I hear footsteps and quickly move to the hole. Hemot, unfortunately, had the same idea, and our heads collide. I back away, and Marleet leans in. She turns back to Hemot with a look of terror on her face. "They're leaving!"

Hemot pushes open the secret door to our little cave and jumps into the hall. Once we're all out, he pushes the door closed and then leads the way back down the hallway toward the servant's quarters.

Before we get far, however, the Captain comes around the corner. He's angry, which is quite typical. I step off to the side of the corridor and bow my head. The other three follow suit.

The Captain stops in front of me and barks, "Caric! What are you doing here?"

"I'm sorry, Captain," I say with as much submission and fear as I can squeeze into my voice. "We are now heading back to our quarters. We have a little more work to do this afternoon."

"You do, do you?" Captain Tilbur says. "I see you working now and then, Caric, and I see the girls working, but I rarely see Hemot working." He steps over to Hemot and growls out the question, "What is it you do in the castle, Hemot?"

"I deal with the curtains, Captain."

"The curtains?" The Captain pauses for a moment. "That's really a full-time job?"

"It is, Sir," Hemot replies. "And I do a fantastic job."

The Captain remains before Hemot for a few more seconds before walking away. When I glance up, I see the Captain shaking his head.

"You know you're supposed to do other work as well, Hemot," Ellcia says. "There's plenty of other stuff that actually needs to be done. You're not just the curtain-guy."

"Nope!" Hemot said. "When I was eight, don't you remember the Steward telling me to take care of the curtains?"

16

I shake my head. "That was supposed to be for one day, Hemot."

"Nope, that was a permanent assignment. He's never given me another job, so I'll continue to take care of the curtains. Just because that gives me plenty of free time every day doesn't mean I'm not doing a good job."

I frown and continue on my way. I like Hemot, but he sure can be irritating.

We wander back toward the third-floor corridor where Ellcia and I are working. We still have a little left to do, and Marleet offers to help while Hemot examines the curtains. I often wonder how Marleet gets so much time away from her kitchen duties, but I never ask.

Just as we finish for the day, Hemot nods at me. I recognize the look in his eye, and I rarely like what comes next, but he's also a lot of fun and my closest friend, aside from Ellcia. I focus on my work as I wait for it to come out.

He nods a few more times, as if I know what he's thinking, but I just grimace at him. I'm sure it'll be fun, but it'll likely be really dumb, too. Finally, he grabs me, pulls me into the center of the corridor and says, "You're right! We need to do this!"

I nod my head and smile. "I'm always right, Hemot. What do we need to do?"

"We're going! We're going to be one of the search parties! We'll be a Vanguard!"

I hear Ellcia laugh behind me, and Marleet gasps. It takes me a moment to understand what he's talking about since it's so ridiculous.

"Hemot, I never..." but I stop myself. There's no point in arguing with Hemot about what each of us said or didn't say. Instead, I focus on what I think I can take care of. "Hemot, I don't think we're search-party kind of people."

Ellcia steps up next to me. "Hemot, he's right. I know you get excited about this kind of thing, but we kind of have a job here and none of us have even been out of the city—at least since we were little kids."

"I know!" Hemot says with a big grin. "That's what makes it perfect!"

I shake my head and take a quick glance at Ellcia. Her eyes are closed, and her head bowed. It's something she does when she's frustrated. She tells me it helps to calm her down.

Marleet steps up next to Hemot and says, "I think we should at least consider his idea."

I know Marleet. To me, she's like a sister—a very close sister. I know she doesn't want anything to do with this Vanguard-thing, but she doesn't want to disappoint Hemot. Marleet is never one for adventure... or danger... or inconvenience... unless it's to help someone. She'd do anything for someone in need. She has a kind heart.

But I see a twinkle in Hemot's eyes and find myself shaking my head again. He's about to lay on the charm.

"Marleet," he says in his kindest voice with his eyes fixed on hers. "Will you go with me?"

"Yes!" she screams without hesitation. She turns back to Ellcia and me and says, "Hemot and I are going on the quest to find the Prince, and we would like the two of you to join us."

I look over at Ellcia, and she's rolling her eyes so hard I instinctively put my hand on her back to steady her. When she's finished, she takes Marleet by the arm, and the two of them walk away.

Hemot turns to me and asks, "So, you in?"

I scowl at him, and he laughs. I think he knows that as bad an idea as this is, I actually want to go.

3

The Quest

I swing my feet over the edge of my bed and drop to the floor. Hemot's already dressed and ready to head to work as the curtain steward, whatever that means. Before he goes, he stops me and tries once again.

"I know we've talked about this a lot the last couple of days, Caric, but today is the only day we can register as an official search party. We need to decide today, or we won't be one of the Vanguards."

I scowl at him. "Hemot, I don't think we know enough about surviving out there to actually... you know... survive. I think the lack of surviving makes me think it's a bad idea—as if we might not... you know... survive." I stop and lean in close before I ask, "What do you think about that whole thing, Hemot? You know, the not-surviving part?"

Hemot laughs. "Marleet and I have already figured all that out. We have a plan. We'll need you to look it over along with Ellcia, but I think it's a good start. Besides, you already told me yesterday that you were considering it."

"Then why do you keep bugging me about it? Why not talk to Ellcia? She's completely against it."

Hemot smiles. "Because Ellcia really doesn't like me. Ever since I asked her out on a date while perched on top of the statue of King Ocnor."

"You think the perching is what turned her off?" I ask, doing my best not to roll my eyes. "Either way. I won't go if Ellcia doesn't go."

Hemot laughs again. "I know that, Caric. That's why I'm talking to you. You are the key. If Ellcia goes, what will you do?"

"I'll go, of course," I say before I can catch myself. The truth is, I'd never stay behind if Ellcia was going. If I'm honest with myself, I'd never stay behind if Hemot went.

"Yep," Hemot says. "That's what I mean. She's the same way. She might try to stop you, but if you decide to go, then it'll be all four of us. Since she doesn't like me very much, I won't be able to convince her. But if I can convince you, we're all set!"

"And why do you want to go?" I swing open the door to our room.

"We're a team, Caric!" He grabs my arm before I can get away. When I turn back to him, he has an intense look in his eyes. The smiles are gone, and he actually looks serious for once in his life. "Caric," he says softly, "we can do this. We don't do anything here. All we do is clean the castle because our parents used to live here. I don't want to…"

Hemot stops, and I'm not sure what to do. I've never actually seen him serious before. I guess I had just assumed it wasn't something he did.

I don't like talking about this kind of thing. Ellcia does now and then, and I talk to her, but it makes me feel things I don't like. The pain wells up inside me as I picture my dad. I don't actually even remember what he looked like, but I know he was tall and strong and no one ever questioned anything he ever said. As I push down the thoughts of my dad, an image of my mom flashes into my mind. I can't see her face, but she's dressed in a beautiful flowing gown and laughing with me.

"But this is where our parents lived," I say quietly. "I don't know if I want to leave. What if somebody comes back for us?"

I had never said that out loud before. I always wondered if I had more family out there. It couldn't have just been my parents. The Regent once told me he was distantly related to me, and that we are kind of like family, but he was always too busy to spend much time with me.

"Then we'll come back," Hemot says. "We'll go out and find the Prince. Once we've found him, we'll come back, and the Prince will be so happy he'll track down any family we might have."

At that moment, something changes inside. I'm not sure exactly what's happened, but I know it's time to do something different. It's time I stop living in the castle. It's time I stop doing what's safe. I smile at Hemot. "Okay. I'll go!"

Hemot laughs, gives me a hug, and announces, "We have a leader!" and runs off.

"Wait, what?"

I catch up to him just as he finds Ellcia, standing in the General's Ballroom. We should have had it finished by the end of the day yesterday, but there was a mess in one of the Lord's rooms, and Ellcia and I had to take care of it.

Hemot rushes up to her and wraps his arms around her. After pushing him away, she glares at him before putting her hands on her hips. "What are you doing, Hemot?"

"We're going!"

She rolls her eyes as she often does in Hemot's company. "No, we're not!" She turns and continues her tour of the room. She always looks through an area before we dive in. She has a great mind for figuring out details, and I've learned never to question her ability to figure out tasks.

"Yes, we are!" Hemot says. "Caric just agreed."

Ellcia turns to look at me, and I can see she's displeased. I don't want to go without her. I hope Hemot is right, and she'll go if I go. I say as confidently as I can, "I have decided to go. I'd like you to come with me… with us."

She stares at me in shock for a moment before she finally nods. "I figured you would. Okay then, I'll get to work on a list of supplies we'll need, and you lay out our plan for how we're going to proceed."

"What?" I don't know why I'm expected to lay out a plan.

Before Ellcia can answer, Marleet wanders in. "I'm here, Hemot."

Hemot turns to me and says, "I told Marleet to meet us here this morning since I knew you'd agree to go."

"What?" I ask again. "I really don't know what's going on."

"Well, that's a problem," Marleet says with a smile. "You're our leader."

I decide not to ask "What?" again, but instead I ask, "Why do you all keep expecting me to lead?"

"We need a leader for something like this," Hemot explains. "Captain Tilbur won't approve our search party unless we have a designated leader."

"And why me? This is Hemot's idea."

"Oh, no…" Ellcia shakes her head quickly. "If Hemot's calling the shots, I'm not sure any of us will go."

I look at Hemot, and he doesn't look offended. In fact, he looks like he agrees completely.

"I might still go if Hemot is in charge," I say.

"No, you won't," Ellcia says. "Hemot won't even go if he has to lead it."

"Really?" I ask Hemot.

"Oh," Hemot says with a laugh. "Didn't I show you the plan that Marleet and I came up with?"

He hands me a piece of paper. On the top of the page, a short note is written. It reads,

Hemot's ~~Pain~~ Plan
Try to find some horses and then ride toward where the Prince might be. When we find him, bring him back to the ~~castel~~ castle!

"That's not a plan!"

"No," Hemot says. "That's why I can't lead this team."

I turn to Marleet. "Don't you want Hemot to lead?"

Marleet smiles sweetly at Hemot before saying, "Oh, Hemot's a great guy. I mean, I just think he's the most wonderful guy in the world. But he's not a leader. I think if he tried to lead, we'd find ourselves floating in the middle of the ocean, and none of us would even know how we got there."

At her answer, Hemot adds a big nod of his head.

"What about Ellcia?" I ask. "Why don't we get her to lead?"

Ellcia shakes her head. "Nope. I'm good at a lot of stuff, Caric. I know that. But leading is not my thing. People annoy me when they don't do what I think they should do. I also find that what I think people should do usually turns out pretty bad later. I don't have the patience to lead people. You do it."

"What about…" I turn to Marleet. Ellcia tenses up, and a look of terror fills Hemot's eyes. I know Marleet as leader is a terrible idea, but I just don't want to do it.

Marleet smiles sweetly at me and comes and gives me a hug. "Thank you for considering me, Caric. But when we're out there, whoever is in charge is going to have to make decisions about life and death. The wrong decision could mean one of us might die. I don't want to have to live with that kind of thing on my conscience. I think you should lead."

I shake my head and holler, "WHAT?"

"It's you," Hemot says. "Whether you like it or not, you're in charge. Lead us on, Leader Caric!"

I scowl at each of them, but it only seems to make them laugh.

"Fine!" I'm about to suggest that we get some armor and some food for the journey, but I think it through. There's no point in preparing for the journey if we don't have permission to go. No one leaves the city without written permission. Travel is heavily restricted throughout the nation—especially in and out of the city—because of the Regent's care for the people. On top of that, if we were to leave our duties without proper permission, they'd charge us with treason. "Then we'll head down right now to talk to Captain Tilbur. He should be at the castle gate by now."

Hemot cheers, and Marleet smiles as Ellcia steps up close to me. I feel a lot better when she's there. Hemot and Marleet are great, but I never know if I can count on them. They mean well, but they're both a little all over the place. Ellcia will always come through for me.

We move out of the General's Ballroom and into the hallway. The Ballroom is near to the main servant doors of the castle, and the guards barely pay any attention to us as we walk out. We've lived in the castle longer than many of the guards have served as soldiers, so we're rarely questioned at any entrance or exit.

We move through the castle grounds, past the six fountains and along the roads and paths leading to the outer wall surrounding the expansive courtyard. The open area around the castle is designed to function as a keep within the city. Because of this, there's plenty of space both inside the castle and outside, and the walls around the grounds are just as tall as the main walls around the city.

When we reach the wall, we walk through the open gate. Few people move through the gates except for those who live in the castle, or those who are visiting Lords and Ladies. The men standing guard give us a quick glance, but then ignore us.

On the other side, a crowd of people stand in the street near where Captain Tilbur and a few other soldiers have stationed themselves for the day. When I see the Captain, the full weight of the situation falls on me, and I nearly groan. As much as the Regent seems to like me, Captain Tilbur despises me. Some of his closest soldiers and officers under him despise me as well. It looks like the four men standing with him are some of the ones who hate me the most.

This will not be fun.

I lead the way to the Captain. No one stands in line to volunteer at the moment. The crowd appears to have assembled for no other reason than to watch.

The Captain sees me coming, and his face fills with anger. I have no idea what I did to upset the man, but he's hated me ever since I can remember.

"Keep walking, Caric!" Captain Tilbur orders, and the men behind him laugh.

I almost obey but then come to a stop in front of him. The others, I believe, are somewhere behind me. I gather my courage and say, "Captain, we want to volunteer to be one of the search parties. We would like to be a Vanguard."

The Captain stares at me for what feels like an eternity. His expression is completely neutral. I've never seen him look at me that way before. I think I almost prefer the anger. I refuse to budge, however. I remain where I am and await his answer.

When he finally speaks, the answer is simple. "No."

The men behind him laugh again, and one even places his hand on his sword in a threatening manner. I know they won't injure me. The Regent has never approved of soldiers harassing the servants.

"Captain." I do my best to keep my voice steady. I feel anger mixed with terror bubbling up inside. I wish Ellcia was standing next to me, but I don't feel like I can turn around and pull her close. I would even take Hemot or Marleet. "The order sent out about the Vanguards stated anyone could volunteer." I don't want to spell it out for him. He has no actual authority to refuse us.

"It's true," Captain Tilbur says. "But you are a special case. The Regent has taken a liking to you, Caric. If I refuse you, you'll have to go to the Regent to complain, and he'll never approve you to leave." He leans forward as if to add to the effect and whispers, "Never." The men behind him laugh again. They've laughed at me a lot over the years.

I search my mind for ideas. I think he might be right. I can't help but think the Regent won't let me go. He's always talked about how happy he is to have me in the castle. To head out into the Talic Region will be dangerous. It's doubtful the Regent will approve it.

"Captain," I say calmly and take a step forward. I make it clear that the conversation is only for the two of us, but he won't allow it. He waves the other men forward with a large smile on his face. I take a deep breath and continue. "You know that the two of us don't get along. If you approve us, it'll get me out of your hair." I immediately regret saying that as my eyes drift to Captain Tilbur's nearly bald head.

He growls his response and shakes his head. "I'm not a fool, Caric. I might bark at you every time you come within sight of me, but I'm not going to send you to your death. I have approved three Vanguards already this morning. I'm in no shortage of people who want to go find the Prince. Not one of you has reached his or her eighteenth birthday. None of you have left the city since you were children. Do you think you're up to facing off against a Talic Wolf? What about a Reber Troll? You ever meet one? Do you know what to do? If you don't, you'll regret it until it kills you."

I glance back at the others. I've heard of a Talic Wolf and a Reber Troll, but I have no idea what to do if I meet either. The most dangerous animal I can ever remember seeing was a bucking horse. I stayed clear of it. From the looks on my friend's faces, none of them know how to respond.

"I don't know what to do," I say, turning back around, "but I'll find out before we leave."

"No!" the Captain says and turns around, but a commotion a short distance away draws his attention back as people run to get out of the way. Someone or something is coming.

Around the corner comes Rulf, barreling through a man too slow to move in time. Right behind him is Mic. Rulf looks angry, but Mic looks unconcerned. Mic's rarely concerned about anything.

They run in our direction, but I don't think Rulf knows we're here. He's running from something. Whatever he's running from, I wouldn't want to meet it. Rulf is scary enough.

Six men come around the corner. I recognize the one. He's a Baker named Erork from down near the market area. He's never happy, but I haven't seen him angry before. The five men trailing behind are a couple of his sons and three other men whom I don't recognize. All the men either have clubs or swords in their hands.

As Rulf passes by us, his eyes land on me and then on Captain Tilbur. He stops, grabs Mic by the shirt, and yanks him around, depositing him right in front of the Captain. He then growls, "We want to join this group."

The Baker slows down when he sees the soldiers but doesn't back away until Captain Tilbur puts his hand on the hilt of his sword and frowns at the man. After a moment, the Baker takes a few steps back and lowers his own sword. If there's one thing everyone knows about Captain Tilbur, it's that no one messes with him and lives.

The Captain turns back to me for a moment, then turns his head to look at Rulf. A smile creeps up on his face. "You want to be a part of this Vanguard?" he asks Rulf.

Before he can answer, Mic blurts out in his slurred and awkward way, "Join in. Join in."

Captain Tilbur stares at Rulf and Mic like he's considering it. I can't let this happen. We can't go on this quest to find the Prince with Rulf and Mic. I'm not sure we'll survive that. Rulf is likely to beat us all up or maybe even eat us.

"Captain," I begin, "I'm not comfortable with…"

"Caric!" Captain Tilbur hollers. "I didn't give you permission to speak!"

I hadn't realized that I needed permission to speak and almost tell him that, but I decide to hold my tongue. He looks extra grumpy and somewhat confused. A confused soldier is not someone to mess with.

The Captain turns back to Rulf, points at Mic, and asks, "You taking that one with you?"

"Yes, Sir," Rulf growls.

The Captain steps up to Rulf and grabs him by the scruff of his neck. He leans in close and starts hissing in Rulf's ear. I can't imagine why Rulf is putting up with it. The guy doesn't normally put up with anything, but this time he just takes it. It looks like the Captain is chewing Rulf out for something. At one point, Rulf's eyes drift to me, and he stares at me for a moment before turning back to the Captain.

The Captain straightens up and steps back to me. He asks me in his typical angry voice, "You really want to go? You really want to be a part of a Vanguard?"

"I do, Sir," I say, although I don't mention that I'd never want to go with Rulf.

"Then here are the conditions. You'll be a Vanguard of six: the four of you and the two of them. Rulf will be in charge, and all six of you will have to travel together."

When I start to object, his eyebrows go up in a simple gesture. It's not much, but it's enough to remind me I have to agree or not go. I turn back to Ellcia, Hemot, and Marleet. The looks on their faces tell it all. None of them want to go with Rulf—especially if he's in charge. I'm not sure what to do at first, but I know that I still want to do this. If the Prince is out there, we have to do our part. Even if it means traveling with Rulf.

I say to my friends, "I want to go."

The three of them stare at me like I'm crazy, but eventually Ellcia nods. "Okay. Then we go."

Marleet turns to Hemot. I know she'll go or stay, depending on him. Although he was the original driving force, he really doesn't look convinced that we should go anymore. I remember why. Hemot has not had many run-ins with Rulf, not compared to me, that is, but the few times he and Rulf faced off against one another, Rulf was not kind.

I know the Captain is only doing this because he hates me. It's a well-known fact that I'm one of Rulf's favorite targets. Tilbur is probably hoping that I won't make it back.

Hemot finally nods his head, and Marleet grabs his arm and adds her own nod. I turn back to the Captain and agree to go with his conditions.

In a similar fashion to how he had grabbed Rulf, he takes hold of my shirt and pulls me in. When I'm close, he hisses in my ear, "You listen to Rulf, you hear?"

"Yes, Sir," I whisper back.

"And Caric," he says in a growl too quiet for anyone else to hear, "If you really want to go, don't let the Regent know you're going. He'll put a stop to it. He likes to keep you close." He pushes me away, and the other soldiers laugh.

Captain Tilbur turns and makes his way to a small table. I follow him and so does Rulf. The big kid eyes me with a spiteful look and steps just in front of me. I decide to step around him and watch what the Captain is doing. Rulf terrifies me, but I'm not going to let the big guy treat my friends like he treats me. If I'm not leading the group, I'm going to at least let Rulf know I won't back down.

Captain Tilbur drafts up our traveling papers with all our names on it. He knows each one of us from the castle, and everyone knows Rulf, but he asks what Mic's name is. I notice that Rulf's name is at the top of the traveling papers with the word "Leader" written beside it. I want to complain, but I know it'll do no good. At the bottom, the destination is listed as Morgin City. If I remember right, out of the major cities in the Talic Region, that's the most northern fortified city.

When the Captain finishes, he hands the paper to Rulf and says, "Rulf! The papers say you have all five of them with you. I expect you to keep them safe—all of them!"

Rulf grunts a reply. I'm surprised about two things. First, I'm surprised that the Captain thinks Rulf has it in him to protect someone, not just beat them up. Second, I'm surprised that the Captain cares if we live or die.

Captain Tilbur then turns to me. "Listen, Caric. Don't you go wandering off by yourself or take those three with you anywhere, unless Rulf goes with you. Rulf is the one who carries the papers. If you're caught out there alone without papers by a soldier, you'll get arrested, and the Regent won't be around to bail you out."

Before I can come up with a reply, Captain Tilbur stands and walks past all of us. He calls out to the Baker who remains just on the edge of an alleyway, not far away. "Listen up, Erork! These six are now the final Vanguard I'm sending out to search for the Prince. I expect you have some quarrel with Rulf, but that quarrel is ended. If anyone raises their hand against one of the Regent's Vanguards, I'll put a noose around his neck myself!"

"Rulf stole bread from me and on his way out, he dumped my cart into a pile of manure!" the Baker hollers. "Now I have to sell my bread at half price!"

I open my mouth to say something, but then close it again. I'm quite disturbed by what I just heard, but I'm not sure if that's just because I live in the castle. I know we get to eat better food than many people. Maybe manure-soaked bread is a little more common among the people of the city.

There's a long pause as the Captain just stands there facing the Baker with his back to me. I notice the people standing around appear to be struggling with what they just heard as much as I am. Finally, Tilbur turns around. The look on his face says it all. He's not only disgusted, he's finished with the conversation.

The Captain returns to his soldiers, and without looking back he hollers, "You heard me, Erork! Don't mess with them!" He then glances our way and says, "Rulf! Your traveling papers give you permission to go to the armory and take food and supplies from the kitchen. When you arrive at Morgin, you can give the papers to the Lord of the city, and he will help you in whatever way he can. Be gone before the gates close for the night."

The soldiers set to packing up, and Rulf waves us on. As much as I can't imagine this guy as our leader, we have no real choice but to follow.

I'm surprised, however, that he doesn't head to the main gate of the castle. Instead, he heads to the smaller gate by the kitchen. It takes us a while to reach it from that section of the city, but we eventually get there and find the guards are quick to let us through. The four of us, of course, are not a problem, but Rulf's papers erase any doubt for those two.

Rulf leads us directly to the kitchen. I have a little trouble understanding how he knows where everything is, but he seems able to manage well. Mic, on the other hand, looks like he's ready to stumble into everything. He seems fascinated by whatever he sees, and Rulf has to keep grabbing him and pulling him along.

When we reach the kitchen, we step inside. Our papers will allow us to get all the supplies we need, but if the Captain is right that the Regent will never let me leave, we have to hurry, otherwise word might reach him.

I hate sneaking around like this. The Regent has been so good to us, but with every step, I feel more and more committed to finding the Prince. I know that ultimately, this is what the Regent wants.

Tereese turns around and nearly drops the bowl in her hands when she sees us. She sets the bowl down and rushes over. Tereese is not a mean woman. I know she's a kind person at heart, but I've never seen her so much as smile. When the six of us walk in, her face fills with wonder.

I look over at Ellcia, and she's just as surprised as I am. We watch as Tereese comes up to Rulf and places a hand on each of his cheeks. He smiles back at her, and I'm kind of disturbed. I honestly had never thought he could do that with his face.

"Rulfor," Tereese whispers, struggling a little with the name. "Is it really you?"

He nods and grunts a quick response. A tear slowly slides down Tereese's face.

She quickly glances off to the side toward Mic, but then turns back again as if he's entirely unimportant. "Is that the one they call Mic?" she asks with disgust.

Mic steps forward and turns his head and shoulders awkwardly as he says, "I'm Mic. I'm Mic."

I find I can't hold it in any longer, and I ask, "How do you know each other?"

Both Tereese and Rulf turn their heads sharply toward me and nearly growl. I step back involuntarily, and I blurt out, "I don't need to know!"

Rulf reaches up and pulls Tereese's hands off his face and says, "We need supplies. We're heading out. We're the last of the Vanguards."

Tereese steps back and examines each of us, one at a time. Her face is filled with shock, but after a moment she says, "All right. I can help. How long before you leave the city?"

"I hope to be out by mid-afternoon," Rulf says.

Tereese turns around and announces, "Anyone in the kitchen who mentions anything you've seen here or leaves my sight anytime in the next five hours will be on drain duty for a year!"

All the kitchen workers react when they hear Tereese's threat. One man is only two steps from the door but turns around and finds something else to do within sight of the head cook.

Tereese sets to work. She gathers up some bread, a fair amount of cheese, and a few pieces of fresh fruit, but most of what she gathers are things like dried fruits, smoked meats, and nuts. She places everything she collects in two large burlap sacks.

Before we leave, Tereese gives Marleet a long hug and kisses Ellcia on the forehead. She then turns to Hemot, and I watch as she launches into a long scolding about making wise decisions. When she comes to me, she chokes up as she tells me to take good care of the others. She then says goodbye to Rulf and once again ignores Mic.

We leave the kitchens and head down through the servant's quarters. I watch in wonder as Rulf makes turn after turn, leading us on a round-about way toward one of the armories. His path takes us mainly through servant's quarters and some of the less used areas of the castle.

I figure we're going to have to get used to being around each other if we're heading out together. I decide to start that process by asking, "How do you know your way around here, Rulf?"

Rulf grunts at me, then says, "You're not the only one born here, Caric. I lived here until I was nearly five."

I look at Ellcia, and she's clearly as surprised as I am. This means he lived here until around the time of the rebellion. She says, "I'm sorry, Rulf. We didn't know that."

"Wait," I say. "If you lived here until you were five, have you been back since? I don't remember you walking around the castle. How do you remember your way around?"

"Rulf never forgets. Rulf never forgets," Mic says in his awkward way. He then adds, "Don't talk. We have mission. Don't talk. We have mission."

Marleet, ignoring Mic, says, "How come Tereese is so nice to you? Do you know her?"

"Don't talk. Don't talk," Mic says.

I can see Rulf is annoyed, so I keep my mouth shut and so does Marleet. We all continue along the halls of the castle in silence.

Rulf leads us up a flight of stairs, and we find ourselves in a rarely used section of the castle. They only use the rooms in this area for the occasional small meeting when the visitors are not worthy of greater formality.

I'm beginning to think we're going to get through the castle without seeing the Regent when, ahead of us, two soldiers with red sashes across their chests step out.

The Regent's coming.

Before I can do much more than gasp, Rulf swings open a door and runs through, dragging Mic with one hand and me with the other. Marleet, Hemot, and Ellcia run in after us, and Rulf slams the door.

"Rulf!" My heart races, and I have trouble keeping my voice steady. "This is likely the room the Regent's coming to. We can't stay here. We'll be found for sure!"

He grunts at me and then drags both Mic and me to the side of the room. Over the years, I've cleaned this room countless times. There are no hiding places, except under the table and perhaps behind a curtain. But the table's likely to be used, and curtains are never good hiding spots.

I spin around to scope out the room again, hoping to find a spot. Ellcia and Hemot's faces fill with panic, and Marleet looks absolutely terrified. I'm pretty confident from the way my heart is beating that my face doesn't look calm.

I turn back to Rulf, and he's pulling back a tapestry, an ugly one, hanging on the wall. He shoves the edge of it into my hand and orders me to hold it. Behind the tapestry is just a bare stone wall, but Rulf runs his shoulder into it. I'm shocked when the stones move, and Marleet actually lets out a little squeak in her fright.

I would never have thought Rulf would try to smash a hole through a stone wall to provide a way for us to escape, nor could I have imagined that he would be successful. An image flashes into my mind of the Regent walking in while we scramble through a newly created hole behind one of his tapestries.

I hear voices out in the hall and recognize the one as belonging to the Regent. The soldier's steps are near, and we're about to be caught.

Rulf gives another push, and a section of the wall swings inward. Mic immediately runs through, and Rulf grabs Hemot and shoves him in after Mic. He then roughly does the same with Ellcia and Marleet and finally grabs me.

I stumble into a small, dark area, and Rulf steps in after me. He grabs the section of the wall and rolls it back in place as I turn around and take in our new location.

We're in a dark corridor. A small amount of light shines in through tiny holes on the side walls. The floor appears to be made of stone along with the walls. I can just barely make out unlit torches sitting in sconces around head height.

A big shape pushes past me, and Rulf moves toward one of the holes in the side wall. He looks through for a moment before he steps back. I then go over to the hole and peer through. In the room we just exited, the Regent lowers himself into a chair. Across from him, another man sits. The door closes, and I'm just about to pull away, when the Regent speaks up. I don't want to listen in as I would never betray the Regent. Knowing that he won't want me to be a part of a Vanguard bothers me enough, let alone spying on him—well… again… But the first words out of the Regent's mouth make my heart grow cold.

He growls at the other man and leans forward as he spits out, "I want them all dead!"

4

The Armory

The man across from the Regent looks somewhat familiar. I've seen him around before, but I don't know his name. I know he comes and goes from the castle all the time. He simply smiles at the Regent and says, "You know my terms. I'm happy to serve, for a price."

"I'll pay when it's done, Searl!" the Regent barks.

"No," Searl replies. "That's not the way I work."

I feel someone grab my arm, and I almost pull myself away, but then I see it's Ellcia. In the darkness, she points down the corridor. Hemot and Marleet, along with Rulf and Mic, have already moved on.

I follow, trying to make sense of what I've seen and heard. The Regent has been nothing but kind and gracious with everyone. The last time he had anyone killed was when he hanged the rebels after they murdered the king. The Regent even shared with me once that he would rather have jailed them than take their lives, but the people had demanded blood for their king.

I push the whole matter to the side while I try to keep up with the others. Even though it's a stone floor, we still need to be quiet. I fear someone in one of the rooms will hear us. I don't know what might happen if we're caught, but I don't want to find out.

Rulf stops after a little bit, and we all come up behind him. He peers through a small hole for a moment and then puts his ear to the same hole. Once he seems satisfied, he sticks his hand into a small crack in the wall and pulls. There's a slight creak as the wall swings into our dark corridor.

I step up close and see the inside of another tapestry. I wonder how many tapestries have secret doors behind them and how Rulf knows of them, but I don't ask. I've lived in the castle since birth. How could it be that I had never even heard of such a thing?

Rulf slowly pulls the hanging tapestry back and peers into the room. Wherever we are, he's worried we'll be caught.

He pushes his way through, and Mic follows without hesitation. Before Hemot moves through, he looks back at me. Even in the dim light, I can make out the big smile on his face. He's having a great time.

Marleet follows after Hemot. She's breathing heavily. I know it's not from the running. The poor girl is terrified. Ellcia goes next. She looks more annoyed than anything. Not much scares her, but I know she would never want to be caught.

I push through the tapestry, and Rulf shoves me roughly to the side while he reaches through to pull the door closed. He then turns around and rushes past me.

I glance around the room, and my heart nearly stops. The place we're in... it's huge. To my right, on the one end of the room, is a large set of double doors made of oak. The design is intricate, but solid. The room itself is just as beautifully designed as the door. It's longer than it is wide and along the long edge of the room are rows of beautifully shined suits of armor and stone statues of kings from days gone by. Everything in the room, from the tapestries to the tiles on the floor, is all designed to draw one's attention to my left where, placed near the back wall on a platform reached by climbing seven steps, sits an empty throne.

I have been in the throne room many times, but never without an armed guard with me. The room is sacred. If you're in here without permission, the penalty is death. Part of the requirement for an armed guard is to remind us of how important the room is, but the other part is to remind us that no one is ever to sit on the throne except the king.

I have never told anyone this, but I remember being in here once with my dad before he was killed. He let me hide in the room while he searched for me. I know he was an important man in the kingdom because no one questioned him—ever. At one point, while his back was turned, I ran up the steps and sat down on the throne.

My dad had scolded me for doing that, but I remember seeing a certain twinkle in his eye that let me know he wasn't upset. He told me it was natural to want to see what it felt like. He even hinted that he might have done the same thing when he had been my age. I had never told anyone about that day—not even Ellcia. I was afraid I'd get in trouble. I feared when the Prince returned, he would be angry.

But at this moment, it all seems so silly.

"Caric!" Ellcia hisses.

I look around, and I'm shocked to see Rulf detaching a sword from one of the suits of armor. I run over to him and whisper, "Rulf! No, you don't understand. This isn't the armory. You can't take this stuff. This all belongs in the throne room. They'll charge you with treason for taking even a tassel from a tapestry!"

Rulf ignores me until he has the sword strapped securely at his waist. When he's finished, he turns to me and grunts before saying, "This doesn't belong here. This belongs to me. It's mine. It was stolen by the Regent."

I open my mouth to answer, but I'm distracted by Mic. He's climbed the stairs and has grabbed a short sword from beside the throne while saying, "I want this. I want this."

I rush forward to stop him. I don't think it's any worse to take the King's sword than it is to take one from on display in this room. Either theft would carry with it the penalty of death, but it just seems more wrong to me to steal that sword. Besides, I think I can physically stop Mic, whereas I have no hope of stopping Rulf. Before I get two steps, however, Rulf grabs me and says, "If he wants that sword, he'll take that sword!"

I realize I have no choice but to allow it. If Rulf makes a scene, the soldiers who are undoubtedly standing guard outside the room will rush in and arrest us. We'll each die for our crimes. At least if I stay quiet, we might make it out alive.

I nearly groan out loud at what happens next. Once Mic has the sword in hand, he drops down onto the throne and takes a look at it. His face breaks out in a large grin. He looks at Rulf and says, "I like sword. I like sword."

"Then it's time to leave," Rulf says quietly. He lets me go and growls, "This way!"

Rulf runs across the room to a large painting on the wall. He grabs it and swings it around to the right. I had no idea the painting was on hinges. I glance at Ellcia, and she looks just as surprised.

Behind the painting is a solid stone wall with no sign of a doorway. Without a moment's hesitation, Rulf pushes on a stone about chest height and a small door opens. The door is about the size of my shoulders—and I'm not an overly large guy. I wonder how the average man would get through it. It's also high enough that I think we're going to struggle to get through.

By that point, Mic has reached us, and Rulf grabs him and shoves him into the hole. Without asking, he picks up Marleet and tosses her in. She lets out a little scream as she disappears from sight, and I turn to the door. It wasn't loud, but I hear upset voices outside. They don't sound like they're concerned, but they're likely discussing whether to open the door and check.

Rulf notices it too and grabs Hemot and tosses him in after. He's carrying one of the sacks of food that Tereese gave us, and Mic had the other one. I'm surprised that neither sack spills open. I expect Tereese tied them well.

I hear Marleet grunt when Hemot flies through the little doorway and think about how it's only going to get worse. Ellcia goes in next. I'm sure she'd be arguing with Rulf if it weren't for the guards just outside the room.

My heart goes cold as I notice the voices of the guards just got louder. At least one of them has turned toward the door.

I feel my feet lift off the ground, and I go sailing through the small opening. I hit something hard and realize that Ellcia and the others must have scrambled to get out of the way. I feel hands grab me and pull me along. It reminds me that Rulf is sure to follow.

I wriggle out of the way just as Rulf squeezes into the tiny passageway. Once inside, he spins himself around and pulls the picture over the hole just as I hear the footsteps of soldiers in the room.

None of us move, and Rulf doesn't close the stone door. At first, I want him to slam it shut, but then I catch myself. It didn't make much noise when it opened, but it would be enough to alert the guards to our location.

We wait while the guards search the room. I'm hoping that neither of them notice the missing swords, and

I almost laugh when I hear them close the door behind them. They must have satisfied themselves that no one was in the room and left.

I breathe a sigh of relief, and Rulf quietly swings the stone door shut. We're in complete darkness. Even through the small cracks around the door, no light shines through. I figure it's the painting that's blocking any light from that direction.

I feel Rulf move up next to me, and he grunts, "Whoever this is, follow me."

I scramble around and hiss to everyone, "Follow Rulf, everyone."

"Which way?" comes a whisper that I'm pretty sure belongs to Marleet.

"I think there's only one way to go," I say, "but try to follow the noise we make as we crawl."

The tunnel is high enough that we can manage on our hands and knees, but if I raise my head, it scrapes on the roof above me. We crawl for a while, but it's nice and cool in the tunnel, so I don't mind so much. I'm filled with wonder once again that I had no idea this or the other tunnel were here. I had thought I knew every corner of the castle. I have been in every room, or so I thought, and cleaned just about everywhere, even the Regent's bedroom.

My heart feels like it sinks into my stomach as I remember the Regent's words. I want to find some other meaning for what he said, but it is hard to find good in a phrase like, "I want them all dead!"

My head bumps into something, and I back away quickly, thinking I just ran into Rulf's butt. Unfortunately, that was a bad move as I run butt first into what feels like the top of someone else's head. I whisper an apology, and they apologize back. But then I'm distracted by movement ahead. I can just make out the shape of an opening. Rulf and Mic have climbed through. I follow after them and step down onto a stone floor. A moment later, all of us are out of the tunnel and in another hidden corridor. Rulf leads us to the left.

After just a few steps, Rulf grabs something on the wall and starts to climb. When I get there, I see it's a solid wood ladder. We climb for a long time—I'm guessing we've gone up at least a couple levels—before he leads us off to the right into another tunnel.

Around a corner, I see plenty of light through tiny holes shining in from rooms on either side of this passageway. Rulf walks ahead just a short way and peers through one of the holes. He then pulls a handle on the wall, and a doorway opens through which he and Mic step. I follow through, brushing off dust and notice everyone else is doing the same. Most of us look pretty terrible, but Marleet looks the worst. She always wears a beautiful dress whenever she can, but it appears as though a dress like that does not fare well in tunnels and dusty places. She looks ready to cry, so Ellcia puts her arm around her and tells her not to worry about the dress. I almost add in a comment about how she won't be looking her best on the journey ahead, but catch myself. It's probably not helpful.

Rulf grunts, and we follow him around a corner. I'm surprised to find we're in the northern wing of the castle. I keep losing track of where I am with the tunnels.

He wanders around another corner, and the rest of us stay close. Hemot shifts the sack of food over to his other shoulder. He looks unimpressed that he has to carry it, so I steer clear of him. I don't really want to carry it myself, but I know if he asks me, I'll say yes.

We enter a large doorway and Ellcia, Hemot, Marleet, and I come to a halt. I had not expected to end up here.

The room we've entered is called "The Forgotten Armory" because it's just that—forgotten. On the official records and when the castle is being toured, everyone talks about the six armories—which includes this one—but no one's ever brought to see this place.

Most of the swords here are chipped or broken, and the armor is old and rusty. And no one, absolutely no one, uses the place. The room doesn't even get cleaned, which is evident by the spiderwebs and cobwebs in every crevice and corner. The only one who ever comes here is Hob. He's the old soldier who oversees the Forgotten Armory. I only know his name because they mention him now and then, and I've seen him around, but I've never met him.

Sleeping in a chair in the middle of the room is a man far too old for most people to have continued living. Somehow, the man sprawled out before us has managed it successfully.

"Wow!" Marleet whispered. "I don't think I've ever seen a man that old before."

I just shake my head. I wonder if we should wake him or just get what we need and leave.

Rulf clears his throat, and Hob opens his eyes. The old man stands up straight and moves like there's far more energy in him than is natural. He smiles to show a set of nearly perfect and entirely present teeth and lets out a big cackle.

"You've come!"

None of us know how to respond. I'm not surprised that Ellcia, Hemot, and Marleet look to me, but I don't expect Rulf and Mic to. I step forward and say, "We have."

My face goes red. I'm sure there was a better thing to say, but I'm not cut out for speeches.

The man runs right up to me and brings his face in close. Our noses nearly touch, and I can smell his breath. Something inside that man's gut is not right.

"Didn't we fight together in the Battle at Reber's Gate?" he asks me. "I think you were in charge. Yes, I remember you. You were there, and you led us to victory."

"I think you have me mixed up with someone else," I say awkwardly. "We're here for some armor."

The man frowns and says, "Orders, please."

Rulf hands him the paper from Captain Tilbur, and Hob runs out of the room and stands by the window. He holds the note up to the sunlight and examines it closely. After a moment, Hob runs back, hands the paper to Rulf and then circles each of us, one at a time. As he moves, he looks us up and down and mumbles under his breath. At Marleet, he stops and says, "You will have to take off that dress!"

"What?" Marleet screams, and each of us quickly step next to her.

I'm surprised to see Rulf place himself right between Marleet and Hob. It makes me wonder if this is the way he views Mic. He sees the boy as someone in need.

"No, no, no!" Hob explains. "I don't mean here." His face screws up in some kind of expression that includes a mix of shock and embarrassment... I think.

He peers around Rulf's bulk and says, "I'm sorry, Lady Aldora, but you will have to change out of your dress in one of the change rooms in the back of the armory. You can't wear a dress while you wear any of my armor. It won't fit."

Hob turns around and grabs a tunic and trousers off a shelf that appear as though they'll fit Marleet and hands them to her. He points toward the back of the room and says, "My Lady," before skipping to a shelf with chain mail.

He begins to collect chain mail and leather armor off the shelves and then races them back to each of us. He drops sets of armor down in front of us in clouds of dust, then

45

heads off to find us swords, mumbling about how two of them already have their swords, so he only needs four more.

As Marleet moves off to find her change room, I bend down and take a look at what Hob has left for me. I'm not overly familiar with armor, but I'm disappointed to see that what he picked out is old and well used. My leather armor has cuts and slices in it, although nothing appears to have gone through. I glance around at the others and see a similar reaction from each. Rulf growls in disgust.

"Hob is required to give us the armor we need," I say, "but he's not required to give us nice armor."

"Then we'll take what we want," Rulf says.

"Oh, no!" I say. "If you rob an armory, we'll be arrested." I lower my voice to a whisper and say, "You can't expect to get away with stealing from this room. Not with Hob around."

"Put on that armor!" Hob screams from the other end of the room.

"I don't think we know how," Ellcia hollers back.

The man runs back to us. I have no idea how the guy moves like he does, but he reaches us quickly. He jumps in front of me and starts shoving the armor onto my body, explaining as he goes. I do my best to watch how everything goes on, but he moves fast. He moves on to Rulf, then Mic, then Ellcia, then Hemot. By the time he's finished, Marleet comes out of the change room. She has a big frown on her face and, to be honest, I struggle to recognize her.

I'm not sure I've ever seen her in anything less than something beautiful. What she's wearing at this moment is plain, brown, baggy, and entirely unflattering. To add to it, she's tied her hair back behind her head. Aside from when it's been done in braids, I've never seen her with her hair anything like that.

The three of us stifle laughs while Rulf looks confused. Mic just mumbles, "Girl not happy. Girl not happy," under his breath.

Hob runs for Marleet, grabs her by the arm, and drags her to where he has her armor laid out. When he's finished throwing it on her, she looks far better. I see her touch a small, pretty purple crest near her left shoulder, and a slight smile creeps onto her face.

"Weapons!" Hob hollers and runs off again. He comes back a moment later with swords and bows and arrows and even a crossbow. He grabs a sword and rushes it to Marleet, along with a small dagger. He does the same for Hemot, then Ellcia. Rulf and Mic already have swords, so he gives them each a knife. Finally, he comes up to me and straps the sword belt on me himself, attaching the dagger on my right and the sword on my left.

He comes up right into my face again and whispers, "You have a nice sword."

When he's finished, he offers a bow and arrows to anyone who wants it. Hemot takes him up on it, and Mic takes the crossbow. Mic says to Hob, "Show me how. Show me how."

Hob beams a smile back at him and screams, "Okay! Okay!" A moment later, he's walked Mic through using the weapon.

Personally, I'm terrified at the thought of Mic having a crossbow. At least with a sword, we can stand far enough away from him. But a crossbow is another matter. I had heard that those kinds of things can sometimes punch a hole through plate armor.

When he's finished giving all the instructions, Hob tells Mic to shoot the arrow at a shelf on the other end of the long armory. Mic awkwardly raises it up while saying, "Shoot now. Shoot now." When he releases the arrow, it fires across the room and sinks into the shelf. I don't know if he meant to hit that spot, but he drove it right into a red piece of cloth hanging down. If that was on purpose, then Mic is a deadly shot. If he didn't mean to hit that exact spot, then… well… either way, Mic is a deadly shot.

When we're all suited up and our weapons are secured to our belts and backs, I stop and look around at each of us. Marleet's armor is well fitted and quite nice. She actually looks beautiful in it. Hemot looks dangerous in his armor. It's beat up, but it's obvious that it was expensive and high-quality workmanship. Rulf's armor hangs off his body in a sloppy manner, but it actually adds to the effect and makes him look even bigger than he is.

Ellcia looks stunning in her armor. I catch myself with that thought and feel my face turn red. I actually take a moment and try to figure out if I said what I was thinking out loud. I don't think I did, so I relax.

Mic looks unimportant in his armor. It's as if Hob didn't think Mic was even worth the armor, yet I can tell that it'll offer solid protection. I decide not to worry about him. His armor is so unimpressive, I find it easy to ignore him like everyone else does.

Once I'm done examining the others, I realize everyone is staring at me. I look down at my own armor and realize why they look so embarrassed. I'm wearing what appears to be the poorest made armor imaginable. It's in far worse shape than anyone else's armor, and I'm confident the soldiers in the city and at the gate will laugh at me.

I don't normally like to complain, but I'm not sure I'll even see Hob again. "Hey, Hob!" I begin, trying to sound confident. "Why did you give me this armor? It looks like it's the worst armor in the kingdom!"

Hob responds with an actual giggle. He runs up to me and whispers, "This is why, Sir!" He reaches out and grabs my dagger. Before I can respond, he plunges it into my chest.

5

The Exit

I feel the knife penetrate deep, and I scream. Hob laughs as I go down, and I see my friends run to my side. Even Rulf and Mic seem upset, but I can't be bothered with that for the moment.

Hob is still a threat. I need everyone to take him down before he attacks again, but they just stare at him and me while I gasp for air and cling to life.

Ellcia puts her hands on my face, and I feel tears stream down my cheeks. I can't believe I am going to die at the hands of a man like Hob while he stands there laughing, and my friends crouch around me—doing nothing. I find I'm not actually afraid of death, I just feel such loss that my friends will go on without me. I can't imagine not being there for the rest of their lives.

"Snap out of it!" Ellcia says, holding tight to my head. "You're fine."

I look down at my chest and see there's no hole from the knife, nor is there any blood. As soon as I realize I'm not injured, the pain fades away instantly. My mind shifts back to everything going on in the room, and Rulf grabs me by the leather armor and yanks me to my feet.

Hob comes up to me, and I flinch, but he laughs as he gives me a tight hug. He hands my dagger back to me and says, "I would have thought you'd remember that, your Highness! Perhaps your age is catching up to you. Not like me! It never catches up to me! I'm young forever!" As if to confirm this, he giggles like a little child and, unbelievably, does a cartwheel. He turns back to me and adds, "Your armor is enchanted, my old friend! It may not look like much, but nothing can pierce that leather armor. Nothing!" A strange look of agony comes across his face as he whispers, "If you were wearing this back then… you might still be alive." He turns back to me with a serious look and steps toward me. "But if you forget that you're invulnerable and believe it can hurt you, you'll feel the pain and can even feel the effects of it. In other words… you can die even though nothing has cut into your body!"

I frown at him in the hopes that he figures out how angry I am. "You could have just told me that instead of stabbing me."

"Nope!" Hob says with another giggle. "It's no fun that way." As if to make it worse, he reaches up and boops my nose.

I feel like punching the man, but I hold back. Aside from my fights with Rulf, I've never actually taken a swing at anyone before. Even with Rulf… I've never actually connected a punch.

Hob turns around and walks to the side of the room. He grabs six old packs off the wall and tosses them to us. From the way they land, they already have a few supplies inside. I open one and see it does have some things stuffed in the bottom, although they're not in any order after being thrown across the room. He then runs around and grabs traveling clothes that he thinks will fit us, a bunch of dusty waterskins, and a flint and steel for each.

We immediately begin dividing up the food among the packs. Rulf's pack is the biggest, and he takes the largest amount. Without drawing attention to it, we don't give as much to Marleet. She is, by far, the smallest out of everyone.

When we're finished, Hob steps up to Mic. "Nice sword," he says with his eyes bulging and an awkward smile on his face. "Draw it for me!"

At this moment, I think Hob appears not only mad but also quite dangerous. There's something about him… something that makes him appear… deadly.

Rulf takes a step forward, but Hob merely raises his pointer finger at him, stopping Rulf in his tracks.

"Draw it!" Hob growls.

Mic pulls the King's sword from its sheath, and I gasp. It's… beautiful. But before I can examine it, Hob orders him to put it back. He then demands that Mic take it off for just a moment.

I'm surprised he so quickly obeys. I thought he was pretty committed to keeping it.

Hob takes it from him and brings it to me. "Now… you draw it!"

I take the sword. I want to just hand it back to Mic. The King's sword is… well… kind of sacred. But then again, I'd really like to draw it.

I pull it from its sheath and feel a warmth spread through my hand, my arm, my chest. It feels good. No, it feels more than that. It feels right.

"Yes," Hob says slowly and quietly, "it knows you too." Then, in a loud, formal voice, he orders, "Put it back in its sheath!"

I do, and the sword is wrenched out of my hands and handed back to Mic, who straps it on his waist. When he's finished, Hob moves back and forth between both of us, examining both of our eyes. When he's done, he merely smiles and hollers, "GOOD!" then raises his arms and says,

51

"I wish you all the best on your quest and hope that you find more than what you are looking for! Some of your armor and weapons are enchanted, but I think it's more fun to let you all figure out for yourselves which pieces are enchanted and in what ways. And…" he says with a little giggle, "I picked the armor I have given to you so that no one will take you seriously."

I frown at that, and so does everyone else. The sight of our reaction just seems to excite Hob more.

"Your armor will not attract much attention. I think that's what the six of you want, right?"

I almost correct him. There are only five of us, but then I remember Mic. He's certainly not an important member of our Vanguard. I don't know if I've ever even heard him speak before. We'd probably be best just to leave him behind. I mean… what's he got to offer?

I nearly groan as I realize what's happening. Mic's armor is enchanted to make people not take notice of him— I couldn't even remember hearing his voice for a little bit there. I hope we can learn to look past the enchantment ourselves because it's going to be annoying to keep forgetting about him.

"Rulf and my friend!" Hob says in a quiet, intense voice as he grabs my and Rulf's arms. "Get out of the city quickly. Don't be noticed. Take the Southern Gate. No one will think to look for you there."

Ellcia glances over at me in confusion. "Are we in danger?"

Hob's smile disappears, and for the first time since we walked in, he looks genuinely sad. "From this moment on, dear Lady Ellcia, you will never stop being in danger. Remember who this is about. There is nothing more important than ensuring the Prince's safety." He then turns in a circle, sits down in his chair, and in a few seconds, he's snoring again.

We all stare at Hob for a moment. It's as if we're sure there's supposed to be more. After a few seconds, Rulf grunts, "Let's go." He picks up his pack, secures it on himself and then helps Mic with his.

The rest of us scramble to get our packs on and then follow Rulf out of the armory and down a flight of steps. I've never worn anything like the pack before, and it's not long before it hurts my shoulders. I can see Ellcia's dealing with the same thing, and I step up next to her.

"You okay?"

She grimaces, shakes her head, and then asks, "You?"

I shake my head back and let out a little laugh. "No. The armor is hot, and it's weighing me down. The pack hurts my shoulders, and I want to take a break. We haven't even gotten out of the castle, and I want to quit."

She smiles at me and says, "I don't want it to be hard for you, Caric, but I'm glad I'm not the only one feeling that way."

I'm content to let Rulf lead as he seems to know the castle better than I do, which I still don't understand. He leads us down to the bottom level and by the soldier's barracks. I think for sure that they'll harass us, but they just laugh at our armor and then forget about us. I guess Hob was right. I wonder if we had shiny armor, if we'd face some difficulty.

We end up outside to the north of the main courtyard. I look around anxiously in case the Regent happens to be out. I feel sick to my stomach. The Regent has almost been like a father to me over the years. No one else seemed to really care about me and how I'm doing—aside from my friends. Now, after all he's done for me, I'm sneaking out, knowing full well that he wouldn't want me to go. I feel like I'm betraying him. But at the same time, I think I'm doing the right thing.

Ellcia pulls me from my thoughts and asks, "What did you think about what Hob called us?"

"What?" I ask, not sure what she means.

"He called you 'Your Highness' and me he called 'Lady Ellcia'. He even called Marleet, 'Lady Aldora'. It's not proper to call us things like that," she says. "Why do you think a soldier would do that?"

I shake my head. "I think he was just mocking us. He's a strange man. Remember, he also thought that he and I fought together at Reber's Gate." I laugh as I think about it. "That battle had to be ten years before I was born. He thought I led that battle. I don't remember who it was, but the man who led them to victory was a famous General or something."

"General Geran. General Geran." Mic says. "Important man. Important man. Died defending the king. Died defending the king."

I'm about to ask Mic how he knows that when we reach the side gate on the north end of the castle. The men don't even look at us, other than to laugh at our attire. They go back to their conversation about something to do with half-priced bread, and we move on.

Once out of the castle, Rulf picks up speed, and we do our best to keep up. With the added weight of the armor and packs, along with the weight specifically on my shoulders, I struggle almost from the first step. After moving down a few streets, I'm about to ask for a break when Marleet beats me to it.

"I can't…" she begins. "I can't continue."

Rulf grunts his annoyance but turns down a small alleyway. He grabs Marleet roughly and checks her pack. "You're wearing it wrong!" he says and starts to adjust it. I watch closely and see that she tied it on like I did. The way she had it, the weight was all on her shoulders, but Rulf ties the belt tight, so all the weight sits on her waist.

I do the same to mine, and I'm happy to find I can breathe a lot easier. My legs are going to tire quickly, but without the struggle on my lungs, I'll manage a lot better. I help Ellcia with her belt and find that Rulf has turned to help Hemot.

When we're finished, Rulf explains, "We need to move. The Captain was right. We must get out of the city by mid-afternoon."

We start out, but Ellcia steps in Rulf's way. "Why?" She asks in that voice she uses when she wants to let someone know there's no other option than to answer her question. "Why do we have to get out of the city so quickly?"

Rulf leans in close to her in a threatening manner. Ellcia steps back, and I step in close to her. "Because, Lady Ellcia," he says, his voice dripping with sarcasm, "the Regent doesn't want you to leave."

"He can find new cleaning staff," she says. "I'm not convinced leaving without telling at least the steward is the right thing to do."

Rulf growls, but Mic comes up next to him. "Be calm. Be calm."

Rulf stands up straight, closes his eyes for a moment, and takes a deep breath. When he speaks again, he sounds like he has composed himself. "The Regent doesn't care about his cleaning staff, Ellcia. He doesn't want any of you to leave. He keeps you for his enjoyment, not for wiping down his statues. Especially that one!" At the last part, Rulf shoves his finger into my chest. It hurts a lot, and I have to remind myself not to believe anything can hurt me through my leather armor.

"Why me?" I ask.

Rulf grunts and turns to leave, but stops. "He doesn't want you to leave, Caric. He likes having all of them around, but you're his favorite. You aren't there because he needs his toilets cleaned. He likes knowing that YOU are cleaning his toilets."

I shake my head and open my mouth to ask more, but I realize I have no idea what to ask. Nothing Rulf says makes sense to me.

"It doesn't matter," Rulf continues. "If you want out of the city, it's now or never."

Rulf turns and rushes out of the alleyway with Mic following close behind. We scramble after him and somehow manage to keep up. He leads us west toward the harbor and then south around the castle, which seems like the wrong way to go, but it's all I can do to keep up with him, let alone convince him to take a more direct route. I expect he's leading us to the southern gate in the hopes that we won't be held up. The eastern gate is quite busy. Maybe that's why Hob told us to head south.

We move along quickly and weave through the city streets. Most people recognize Rulf right away and steer clear of him. He has quite the reputation.

When we're nearly at the gate, someone catches my eye. I recognize him but can't quite place him at first. I push him out of my mind, but it keeps bothering me. I'm just about to ask Ellcia about him when I remember. He was one of the men who had shown up with the baker—one of the men who had chased Rulf.

I'm just about to call out to the others to warn them when a large man steps out in front of Rulf and smashes a long piece of lumber across Rulf's chest. Rulf goes down and two other men grab Mic.

I charge forward and slam myself into one of the men holding Mic before I really think through what I'm doing. The man goes flying backwards, and the impact jars me enough that I land on the ground. It takes me a moment to figure out what's going on, but by the time I do, someone has me in a grip.

I twist around and catch sight of Mic again. The boy is staring at Rulf on the ground. Mic's face fills with rage, and he twists around, driving his fist into the chin of the man holding him. The man goes down, and Mic is free.

The man holding me, however, has me in a grip of iron. I struggle against him, but it seems to do nothing. Ellcia comes to my rescue, and the man just tosses her aside.

Hemot and Marleet run to help me as well, but the guy who has his arm around me is huge. A moment later, Hemot is held by another man, while Marleet hits the ground next to Ellcia. I struggle as hard as I can, but it makes no difference.

I'm amazed at Mic. He fights like a wild man. His sword is out, but he appears to be trying not to hurt anyone. He strikes the man who had held him with the flat of the sword, and the man backs away.

I find myself spinning around, and I hit the ground hard. I look up in time to see Rulf is back on his feet and angry. The man who had me in his grip has just taken a punch to the gut, and he goes right down. Once he hits the ground, he just lays there and groans.

One by one, Rulf takes down all the men. It turns out there's four of them, and even when two men attack him at the same time, Rulf doesn't struggle at all. Once the men are all down, he hollers to us, "Get up! We're nearly at the gate!"

I scramble to my feet and help up Ellcia and Marleet. They both look dazed, but Ellcia's angry. Mic helps Hemot, and the five of us… or… the six of us… set out at a near run—or as fast as we can move in our armor and with our packs.

I glance back to see three of the men have resumed their pursuit and have been joined by the Baker. The Baker himself is enraged. The whole pursuit seems overkill to me, but… Rulf has an effect on people.

Ahead, the gate comes into view. It's well guarded, as no one is allowed to enter or leave the city without permission. We run up and stop in front of the guards. They look at us with irritation, but they eye the men behind us with anger. The baker and his friends stay back, likely waiting to see what will happen to us. If we're turned back into the city, the guards won't do anything to stop the three men— although I'm not too concerned now that I can see what Rulf can do. And Mic isn't a bad fighter either.

"What do you want?" a small guard asks. His armor declares him a Sergeant. I know all the soldiers at the castle, at least by sight, if not by name, but this man is entirely unfamiliar to me.

Rulf gives his regular grunt for a response and hands over our papers. The man reads it and then turns it over and reads the other side. I hadn't known there was anything on the other side. He asks each of us our names and then confirms where we're heading. Rulf growls out the words, "Morgin City," and the Sergeant nods before waving for us to follow him. He hands the papers back to Rulf before leading us through to the other side of the open gate.

Once there, the Sergeant turns to the rest of us and laughs. He focuses in on me and says, "You're heading out into the country wearing armor like that? Have you ever even drawn your sword?"

The truth is, I haven't. Aside from when Hob helped me strap it on, I haven't even touched the grip, nor have I seen the blade outside its scabbard. I remain silent, however, unwilling to admit that I've never drawn it or any sword, aside from Mic's.

"No answer, eh?" the Sergeant says. "That either means you're a deadly warrior who isn't threatened by me at all, or you don't want to tell me the truth." He and the men have a good laugh before he adds, "I think we both know which one it is." He leans in close and asks me, "Out there, you're going to have to go through Switcher Pass and then somehow make it through the Talic Region. Do you think you can keep yourself alive?"

Ellcia steps up next to me. She takes my arm and says, "Maybe this isn't such a good idea."

The Sergeant and all the guards laugh even harder at this. He turns to her and says, "Your papers say you can leave the city, little girl. I don't see anything on there about coming back in. You want to turn around now and try to enter the city without permission? You want to find out what happens to people who try that?"

Ellcia's face drains of all color, and she quickly shakes her head. The guards laugh yet again and turn back toward the gate.

Rulf takes off at a fast pace down the empty road, but I rush up beside him. "Hey, Rulf," I say, trying to keep my voice steady. The two of us have never really gotten along. It's been more of a relationship where he punches me, and I try to get away. I think about how he's one of the last people in the entire nation of Sevord that I'd like to be traveling with.

Rulf grunts a reply, and for the first time, I notice that he grunts a lot. I guess I had just gotten used to it.

"I don't think the rest of us can keep up this pace. I'm already exhausted from the trip through the city."

I glance back and realize that out of the four of us from the castle, I'm actually doing the best. Since I've spent so much time running for my life from Rulf—an average of three or four times a week—I figure I've had the most exercise out of any of my friends.

Rulf's response is simple. "Put up with it."

I look back again at my friends. The expressions on their faces let me know that putting up with it is not an option for much longer. We're simply not soldiers and not ready to travel like this.

I rush forward and get in front of Rulf, turning around to face him. My biggest worry is that he won't stop, but he does.

Before I know what's happening, he's grabbed me by the leather torso of my armor and lifted me right off the ground. At first, I fear he's going to toss me off the road into the trees. We're still in sight of the walls, but I doubt the soldiers will do anything to help me. If there was ever doubt in my mind, it's gone. Rulf definitely has giant blood in him.

"We can't slow down, Caric!" Rulf says. "Don't you understand what's happening here?"

Something in his voice causes me to pause for a moment. I thought we were just trying to find the Prince. I thought the rush was because the Regent might stop us. "I don't think I do understand. Can you… um… put me down and tell me what's going on?"

He drops me. He only had me a short distance above the ground, but the weight of the armor and pack, along with how tired my legs are, leaves me crumbling to the ground. Hemot rushes up and helps me to my feet.

Rulf is really agitated. He starts pacing back and forth. I see him glance back to the city walls now and then, scanning them—I assume he's worried about some threat.

"Look!" Rulf says. "I'm not in danger."

"Okay," I say. I'm not sure how else to respond to that. Hemot is still beside me, and out of the corner of my eye I see that he's glanced my way. I, however, keep my eyes on Rulf. I'm doing my best not to appear intimidated.

"Don't you understand?" He's nearly shouting at this point.

I shake my head slowly and say, "Rulf, I'm sorry. I really have no idea what's going on."

Mic comes up beside Rulf. Although it's hard to focus on him, if I concentrate, I can see he's tired but not as tired as I am. "You know. He doesn't. You know. He doesn't."

Rulf growls yet again and then his shoulder's slump, his head dropping to his chest for a moment. After a few seconds, he says, "I'm sorry, Caric."

Again, I'm left with no idea how to respond. Understanding Rulf is like trying to read a different language.

"I'm not in danger because it's hard to hurt me," he says with a look of compassion in his eyes. "If they catch you and the others, they'll kill you all. I might not be able to stop them. They might eventually kill me too, but I'll go down fighting. And a lot of them will die in the process."

"Who's trying to kill us?" I ask.

"Bad men," Rulf says.

Hemot speaks up at that point. "A little more information might help. I suspect anyone who tries to kill us might fall into the category of being a *bad* man."

Rulf turns back to the castle and says, his voice dripping with sarcasm, "You see that place over there? The city? You notice how the soldiers are watching us? They're laughing and joking about us? The longer they do that, the more likely they are to tell people that we left the city. I took us out the south entrance to try to throw our enemies off— it's what Hob was suggesting too. Every second we stand here, we're more likely to be noticed by the wrong person. If you want to live, we need to get out of sight right away."

I nod my understanding of that part, but there's much more I still don't understand. "Should we leave the path and go through the forest?"

"No!" Rulf says in desperation. "Then they'll notice us even more! No more talking. You will move, now!"

He grabs me by the shoulder and shoves me along. The next thing I know, we're all running again. I've never been out of the city, as far back as I can remember, so I don't know where we're heading, aside from south. I vaguely remember learning about fishing villages and industries to the south, but most of what I remember is to the north and east.

The path south looks like it disappears a short distance ahead, and I hope that's a spot where we can take a break. When we reach it, it turns out the path heads down. Rulf reaches the top of the hill and runs down the hill at the same pace.

My friends gasp for air behind us, and even Mic starts to show signs of exhaustion. When the path levels out, Rulf stops, turns around and stares back in the direction of the city. I look back as well and see that the city is lost behind the hill. Once he's satisfied with what he sees, Rulf turns east and heads into the forest. I rush after him, but he stops and growls at us. "Walk where I walk, and walk single file! Don't mess with any bushes or break any branches. Don't leave any sign that we've gone this way!"

I obey what he says, but I'm starting to get worried. At first, I trusted him that he feared for our safety. Even if Rulf was wrong, at least it showed he was concerned for us. But as we move along, stepping on stones and avoiding any area that might leave an indication of where we've gone, the fear grows in me that Rulf is taking us out into the forest to kill us. They say he's part giant, and giants do occasionally eat people. I realize with horror that if he decided to kill us, I'm not sure any of us could stop him. I glance behind me at Mic. He's taken up position at the back of the group. Is he in on it? Does he eat people too?

I shake my head and push those thoughts out of my mind. It's absurd to think such things, but the guy is clearly hiding stuff—whether he means to or not.

He leads us farther into the forest and up an incline. When we reach the top and the ground levels out, we catch the occasional glimpse of the city through the trees. We're about to head deeper into the forest when he stops and tells us all to get down.

I drop to the ground and push off my pack. I'm not sure if we're going to need to run, but I'm confident I can't run with the pack. When I see no one else drop their pack, I remember my food and supplies are in there, and that I'll never survive without it.

While I'm pulling my pack back on, I see what worried Rulf. Through the trees, I can just barely make out movement down on the road. A dozen horses ride by. At one point, there's enough of an opening in the trees that I can make out two of the men. The one is a soldier who often stands guard outside the Regent's office. I know him because he's usually as nice to me as the Regent is. I hear he was one of the soldiers who helped the Regent take back the kingdom from the rebels.

The other man is the Captain—Captain Tilbur.

My mouth drops open. He's hunting us!

I don't get it. He sent us out here and warned us to move quickly. The fact that he's now trying to catch us… it doesn't make sense.

Yet another grunt from Rulf distracts me, and I dare to ask, "Why is the Captain after us?"

"He's not," Rulf says. "He warned me to move fast and to take the southern gate."

"Then why is he chasing us?"

Rulf growls this time. He's apparently angry at me… or more angry than usual. "Caric, pay attention! He's not chasing us. He's gotta do this to keep up appearances. Most of those soldiers are his own. If he doesn't want to find us, he won't."

"What if they see us?" Ellcia asks, crawling up next to me.

Rulf is getting more agitated by the moment. He doesn't do well with questions. Or answers. "I think the Captain would kill the soldiers he can't trust and let us go."

"Why?" I ask. "The Captain is the worst soldier in the entire castle guard!"

"Yeah," Ellcia adds. "He's been meaner to Caric than anyone else."

Rulf turns his head toward me, and I see confusion on his face. When he speaks, he speaks slowly. "That's strange," but then pauses as though deep in thought. Finally, he says in a quiet voice, "Wait, no… that makes sense."

"What makes sense?" I ask, but Rulf jumps up, grabs both Ellcia and me by our packs and yanks us onto our feet.

"Time to move!"

I glance back down at the road, but there's no sign of Captain Tilbur or his soldiers. I feel like my entire life is now no longer simple. It's as if nothing makes sense anymore, and any questions just make it all the more confusing.

I help Marleet as she struggles to her feet under the weight of her pack. She looks exhausted. Her face is flushed, and her hair is entirely out of place. I've never seen her in such a state. Even when she worked in the kitchen with Tereese hollering at her and everyone else, she was always so much more together.

Before we run on, she wraps her arms around me and squeezes like her life depends on it. After a few seconds, she begins to cry softly, but Rulf barks at us to get moving again.

I don't really know what to do for Marleet, but Ellcia comes up next to her, and they walk and run together for the next while. I decide to give them a bit of space, and I move over to check on Hemot. He is, like the rest of us, exhausted and scared, but he's also overwhelmingly excited. He looks like he could break out in tears or laugh hysterically at any moment. I think if one of those is to happen, I'd almost prefer the tears.

Rulf leads us on through the forest, still heading east. I assume if we were to head north just a short way, we'd reach the main road heading through Switcher Pass and could continue on it to the Talic Region, but Rulf seems to be steering away from it. At one point, I see the main road through the trees, but as soon as he sees it, he moves us a little farther south. It would be much easier traveling along the road, but I suspect he's right. Until I get more answers, the only thing I can do is trust him.

Every step hurts. My feet ache. My legs hurt. My hips feel like something is seriously wrong with them. My lower back throbs with pain. My shoulders are sore from where the straps on my pack rub. My mouth is dry from too little water. And the bugs are bad.

I want to say the bugs are biting me more than anyone else, but it's not true. Hemot seems to be getting it worse than me, but Ellcia seems to attract them the most. The insects literally swarm around her. Ellcia is not happy.

Mic seems fine, and I wonder if his armor is helping the situation. If the enchantment distracts the rest of us from noticing him, it's quite possible it has the same effect on bugs. Rulf is also not bothered by them. At one point, we walked through a hornet's nest, and I was stung about six times. I saw a dozen or more on him, and they appeared to be trying to sting him, but he didn't even notice.

Marleet seems to be faring well with the bugs. For some reason, they just seem to ignore her like they do with Mic. I'm glad about that. She's doing worse than the rest of us with aches, blisters, and exhaustion. It's good she gets a break with at least one part of the agony.

I've mostly trained myself to see Mic by this point. With the enchantment on his armor, I had to remind myself a lot at first, but he has slowly started to stand out a bit more. It was as if my eyes were blurry and have now started to take focus.

We traveled late into the night yesterday without much of a break at all. Rulf explained that on the first day, we needed to get some good distance between ourselves and the castle. Every step could be what saves us from being caught. We tried to get out of him why they wanted to catch us so badly, but Rulf just grunted and then wouldn't speak again until well after dark.

When he did call a halt, we had to figure out our meal in the dark and then set out our bedrolls. Since the sky was clear, we didn't put up a shelter, which was just as well with me. I was so tired. The bugs in that area weren't bad either, which was really nice, although when I awoke the next morning, a spider had spun a web and connected it to my nose. The place had been infested with spiders, but very few of them bit.

When we got up this morning, every part of my body hurt. I suggested that we find a place to camp for the day so we could rest up, but Rulf just growled at me, and Mic said, "Must move. Must move."

The nice part, however, was that Rulf had caught some rabbits in snares that he had apparently set at some point during the night. The smell of the rabbits cooking over the fire was enough to raise my spirits, but I still wished for a day to relax.

We are now approaching Switcher pass. Once there, Rulf says we'll continue through the forest as much as possible rather than take the road. However, he tells us that there are some places where the cliffs come together so close that we'll have no choice but to take the road—either that or we'll be walking within sight of the road anyway.

The light is now beginning to fade, and I grab Rulf's arm. He must be getting used to me because he doesn't growl this time.

"We have to stop, Rulf."

"No! We have to keep moving."

"I'm sorry, Rulf, but we can't." I come to a halt, and I wave everyone else to stop. I can see they're a little nervous about upsetting Rulf, but their exhaustion is enough to overcome any fear.

Rulf keeps running for another few steps, but Mic says, "Time to stop. Time to stop," causing the big guy to come to a stop.

At first, he looks angry, but when his eyes land on Mic, his face softens, and he relents. "Okay, but not here. Let's move a little to the south."

I'm not sure why we'd need to do that, but if that's what it takes, I'm willing. We find a small area to camp behind a rise, which gives us good cover from the road.

It's strange to me how capable Rulf is with everything out in the forest. He can find his way; he can set snares; and he can build fires. As far as I know, Rulf has not been out of the city since he was a little kid—maybe not even then. I can't imagine how he could know all this, but I'm still too uncomfortable around him to ask.

Once we set up camp, Rulf heads out to set up snares, and we dig into some of our food. I try to start a fire based on what I saw Rulf do the night before, but by the time Rulf gets back, I'm just annoyed, and I've cut myself twice on my flint.

Rulf sits down and pulls out his flint and steel. I decide I'm not going to be entirely useless, so I crouch down next to him to try to figure out what he's doing.

"What do you want?" he asks me in his familiar, grumpy tone.

"I'm trying to learn."

He looks at me with confusion for a moment, but then starts to tell me what he's doing. He shows me how to strike the flint and talks about how close it needs to be to the tinder. It still doesn't light quickly, but by the time it does, the other four have gathered around. The look on Rulf's face suggests he thinks it's odd that we're all watching him, but when he notices Mic among those gathered around, he holds his tongue.

Once the fire is going, and we've all eaten, I do something I haven't done yet. I pick up my sword from where I had set it when I settled in at the campsite and pull it out of its scabbard. I've never actually held a sword, aside from the King's sword the other day for a few seconds, let alone fought with one. The scabbard of my sword is pretty basic. I'm not sure if it's decent quality or not, but it's definitely ugly. The sword, on the other hand, is a work of art! It's about the length of my arm, from shoulder to fingertips, and has a grip that I can comfortably fit in one hand, but can squeeze my second hand onto it, if necessary.

Along the blade is written a series of words, but I can't read any of them. None of them are faded in the least, but they're clear, as though the sword was just recently made. The language is something I've never seen before, and even the letters themselves are entirely unfamiliar.

"Wow!" Marleet says.

I glance up, and everyone's eyes are on my blade. I hadn't noticed it at first, but my sword is glowing. It's not a lot, but it's there. Marleet grabs her sword and dagger and pulls each of them out to check them, but it's clear right away that her sword isn't glowing. Ellcia and Hemot follow suit, but both are disappointed as well. All of them have beautiful, well-crafted blades, but none of them compare with mine.

Finally, Rulf and Mic draw their swords. Rulf's blade is longer than mine or anyone else's sword. It's also quite wide and looks like it could chop down a tree in one swipe. I wonder if I'd be able to swing it, but Rulf has no trouble with the weight.

He goes through some motions with the sword, and I hear Hemot whistle quietly. Clearly, Rulf not only knows his way through a forest, but can handle a blade.

Mic's sword, however, causes me to shake my head. I saw it briefly earlier, but I guess I didn't really look closely at it. I'm not sure at first what I'm seeing, but the thing is just wrong. Everyone else stares at it as well. It's about the same length as my sword, I think, but it's dark. I wonder for a moment if it's an effect of his armor, but then I discard that possibility. When he holds food or other items, the stuff he holds looks normal.

I put my sword back in its scabbard and wander over to take a closer look. When I get there, I see a bit of what's going on. While my sword glows just a little, his sword seems to suck in the surrounding light. It's made of a black steel. It, like mine, has letters on it, but the letters themselves glow a faint yellow. The rest of the sword, however, draws in the light and is hard to focus on.

"Can I hold it?" Hemot asks. I was wondering if I could see it again as well. As beautiful and impressive as my sword is, Mic's sword, or should I say the King's sword, looks like it was made for one thing and one thing alone—destruction.

"My sword. My sword," Mic says in reply.

A growl from Rulf suggests that we should not question this. I think we might have to get used to the idea of seeing, not touching, that sword.

"Teach them. Teach them," Mic says to Rulf.

Rulf growls, but says, "All right, everyone. I'm going to teach you how to fight with a sword."

My face breaks out in a grin, although I'm not sure if I'm more excited or more terrified. I glance over at Hemot, and see there's no question about it. He couldn't be happier. Ellcia seems curious, and Marleet looks nervous.

Rulf instructs us to put our swords away. He explains that the swords will not only be loud and might attract attention, but we could also do nasty things like cut each other's arms off. I gladly set my already sheathed blade down, and Rulf orders us to find sticks to use instead. We search until Rulf is satisfied with the length and sturdiness of each branch, then he pairs us off with one another. I get Hemot; Ellcia gets Marleet.

He walks us through some forms and teaches us how to stand and more. After a few minutes, I think I'm getting the hang of it, so Hemot and I try to spar. A few minutes after that, I decide I have learned nothing as I rub my hand and Hemot rubs his arm. I don't think either of us managed to block a single strike.

I check out the girls, and they're doing just as badly as Hemot and me. I wouldn't have thought it'd be so hard.

As I watch Ellcia and Marleet try not to hurt one another, Rulf physically yanks me toward him. He growls, "I'll teach you. Mic will teach Hemot."

I almost laugh at the idea of Mic teaching someone, but my own fear of facing off against Rulf keeps my laughter in check. Rulf sets me down, and we head out of the camp. The firelight shines enough on him that I can see clearly, but I start to remember what it's like to stand up to Rulf.

Rulf has his own stick ready and begins to talk me through what I need to do. He scolds me over and over again about the position of my feet or the way I hold my shoulders. I feel awkward and out of place, but I think Rulf seems impressed with me. I've always been a fast learner when it comes to anything athletic.

After a while, I glance over at Hemot and Mic. I'm shocked to see that Mic, as he mumbles his way through everything, is able to hold his sword and move like he knows what he's doing. I turn my head to catch Ellcia and Marleet, standing with a look of horror on their faces. Apparently, they've decided to stop their own practicing to watch me, and the look of horror lets me know that something bad is about to happen.

I see stars as Rulf's stick catches me on the side of the head. I hit the ground and roll over. When I look up, Rulf stands above me with a frown on his face. Leaning in close, he growls, "There's no point in trying to teach you how to fight with a sword if you're too busy checking out the girls to pay attention."

I feel my face turn red as Rulf moves on to Ellcia. He offers to teach her, and in a few minutes, I see that he's just as rough with her as he is with me. He's a good teacher, but he doesn't mind chewing his students out or giving them the occasional whack with his stick.

When we finish, Mic and Rulf look exactly the same, but the rest of us are tired and sore. We have a long way to go before we're good with our swords.

6

Learning

I awake to a sharp pain in my side. Rulf has kicked me, and he follows it up with a growl. Once my eyes are open, he hisses, "Get up!" and drags me to my feet. I grab my sword and pull it out, not sure what else to do. Rulf and Mic run around waking everyone else up, and when the others see me with my sword drawn, they imitate me.

"What's going on?" I ask.

"Someone's nearby," Rulf hisses. "I can hear a change in the forest."

We move into a tight circle with our backs to the embers of the fire. Rulf points off to the north, and we all turn to face that direction. Mic grabs his crossbow and loads a bolt.

I can't hear anything out of the ordinary, but Rulf keeps twisting his head to the left and right as if he's trying to pick up sounds that only he can hear. A few moments later, he hisses, "Get down!"

We all crouch, and to the north I see movement in the early dawn light. I manage to drop a little lower, although I'm not sure who it could be or why they're a threat to us.

The movement takes shape, and I see at least a dozen men. They're all armed with swords and either bows or crossbows. None of them wear a uniform. They're dressed as regular people, albeit in chainmail armor.

We watch as they move slowly through the forest toward the east. Their heads move back and forth as if they're searching for someone, and I get the feeling they're after us. I see movement on either side of me, and Ellcia, Hemot, and Marleet come up beside me.

"Who are they?" Hemot whispers.

I shake my head. "No idea, but I think we don't want to meet them."

I really don't know for sure that they're a threat, but since we had to rush out of the city and then were pursued by Captain Tilbur, I'm left with the impression that there are a lot of people who are not our friends.

Just as the men are about to disappear out of sight, the one in the lead turns around to glance back. My heart feels like it stops in my chest. I've seen that man before. It's the man to whom the Regent said, "I want them all dead!"

The thought that had been growing in the back of my mind... the one that I didn't want to consider... the thought that the Regent might actually be the enemy comes fully into my head. Rulf suggested such a thing already, but I had outright rejected the idea. The Regent has not only been good to me over the years, but he was the one to stop the rebellion. If he had arrived only minutes earlier, he would have saved the King's life. He's the good guy.

And yet, I think he wants us dead.

Once the twelve men are out of sight, Rulf whispers, "Time to pack up."

We start putting everything back into our packs when I ask, "How did you know people were coming?"

"The sounds in the forest changed. There were fewer birds singing in that direction, and I saw a rabbit run out of that area. And… the crickets."

"Crickets?"

"They weren't chirping as loud in that area of the forest."

"You heard the crickets in one area of the forest stop chirping as loud and figured people were coming?" I ask, absolutely bewildered.

He looks at me as he finishes up his packing. "I hate crickets."

I'm not entirely sure that answers my question, but I accept it. At some point, I hope to have all my questions answered clearly, but I don't think today is the day.

Once we're all ready for the day's hike, we set out. Rulf has obviously been up for a while as he's collected two rabbits and a squirrel from his snares and has already skinned and cooked them. He passes out some of the meat as we move through the forest.

Rulf takes us directly north, instead of northeast, as we had been traveling. We cross where the twelve men had walked through the forest and continue north until the sun is well up in the sky. In time, we come to the main road that leads east and west from the city through to Switcher Pass and on to the Talic Region. It's a busy road with plenty of travelers, but we rush across during a moment when there's no one in sight and continue on our way north.

On the other side of the road, Rulf relaxes a bit. Now and then, Mic says, "Talk more. Talk more," and I can see Rulf is trying to make an effort to communicate with us. He doesn't appear to like doing it, though.

"I think we're now far enough away from the men we saw to slow down a bit," he explains. "We'll travel northeast for a little bit and then head east into Switcher Pass."

"Who were those men?" Ellcia asks.

"Assassins," Rulf says.

We walk on in silence for a few steps. I don't want to ask the question, but at first no one else speaks up. Finally, when the silence is killing me, Hemot asks, "Do you have any more of that rabbit?"

"Hemot!" I hiss. "Seriously? Don't you think there's a more important issue right now than food?"

"I'm kind of hungry still," Marleet says.

We stop and pull out some more of the rabbit and squirrel. I'm not a big fan of the squirrel meat, but there isn't much of it anyway.

As we eat, I decide to ask the question no one else seems to want to ask. "Why are assassins chasing us?"

Rulf looks at me with confusion. I see that look from him a lot. I don't think it's because he doesn't understand. I think he's just always surprised when I don't. "Why are the assassins chasing us, Caric? Because they're trying to kill us."

I try not to roll my eyes as I grit my teeth and shake my head. "Yeah, I know that. I gathered that from the fact that they are assassins. I mean, why are they trying to kill us?"

"Didn't you hear the Regent? He said he wants us dead."

I did hear that, but I am still struggling to come to grips with it. "What does that mean?" I ask, but then add, "Wait, I know that means he wants us dead! I mean, why does he want us dead?"

Rulf grunts. "It's not just us. He wants all the Vanguards dead."

My mouth drops open as Rulf stands, preparing to leave. Mic joins him, but the rest of us remain seated.

"Can you tell us why he wants us all dead?" Ellcia asks.

"Because he doesn't want the Prince to take the throne," Rulf replied.

Without intending to, I laugh. It's an absolutely absurd thought, but I see the others aren't laughing. The truth is, I know it's not an absurd thought. I just don't like it.

"Let's move," Rulf orders.

This time, we all jump up and throw on our packs. We head out again and move toward Switcher Pass, slowly moving away from the road.

Marleet is the first to break the silence. She seems to be doing better now with the traveling than she had been at first. "Why is it called Switcher Pass?"

There's a cheerful tone to her voice, and I see she just wants some friendly conversation. I glance back at her, and she smiles sweetly at me. It makes me feel good inside. Marleet has a way of picking up the mood. I'm glad she's with us. I hope she can find some joy in this conversation.

"It's named after a man they called the Switcher," Rulf says.

"What did he do to have a pass named after him?" she asks as she looks all around. She doesn't seem to be all that interested in the conversation, but she seems happy to chat.

"He killed somewhere near a hundred people. Just one at a time, but he killed them. Some while they were traveling alone through this area. Some while they were in their homes. Some even in public settings. All killed with a barbed knife called a switcher. It was…"

"Thank you, Rulf," Marleet says quickly. "I don't need to hear any more of this. I'm fine with only knowing that it's called Switcher Pass."

Rulf looks confused, but he accepts it. He continues in silence until we stop for a mid-afternoon rest.

After a short break, we get back on the move, but Rulf warns us that we have to be more careful over the next while. "We're coming up on the entrance to the pass. The cliffs come in close here, and we'll move within sight of the road. Once in the pass, we can head a little farther north and get away from any travelers."

Through the trees, I see the cliffs. They're huge, and I understand why no one passes over them. The cliffs are like a high wall, forming a barrier on either side and they lead right into the pass. We move quietly through the area and try to stay out of sight of the travelers on the road. Once through the large, natural entrance, we veer off to the north again and move farther from the road.

After about an hour of traveling through the forest, Rulf puts his hand up. I'm not sure what it means, but I come to a halt. When the others see me stop, they stop too, and judging from Rulf's lack of anger, I figure we did the right thing.

I step up next to him and ask, "What's wrong? Crickets again?"

"No," he said, missing any sarcasm in my voice. "The crickets are fine. Look over there."

I looked in the direction he's looking and shake my head. "I see trees."

"Not the trees. Look at the branches on that bush."

"Ahh, yes," I say in a formal voice. "The branches. The branches are always the things I look for first whilst on a forest walk." Rulf doesn't respond, so I add, "I really have no idea what's wrong with the branches."

"Some are broken, and some of the plants are leaning to the side. Someone has moved through this area recently. They were at a run."

I don't know how he figured any of that out, but I follow him as he creeps forward. The others trail behind, and we slowly follow the invisible path left by whoever might have gone through the area.

When we come across them, Marleet screams. I've never seen dead bodies before. I've heard of people dying, but no one I was ever close to has actually died, aside from my parents, of course, but I had been so young that I barely remember them. Rulf creeps through, and Hemot and I follow.

Rulf checks each of the men until he finds what he's looking for. The second last man he checks has something of interest. Rulf holds it up for me to see. It's traveling papers signed by Captain Tilbur.

This was one of the Vanguards.

Whoever killed them had moved fast. I try to figure out what I can, and from what I can see, they had mostly been killed by arrows. Every man has at least one tiny hole pierced through his armor—their attackers used crossbows. There's little doubt in my mind. The assassins we saw earlier found this Vanguard.

I spin around, searching the forest with my eyes. I'm terrified that I might see one of the men taking aim at Ellcia, or Hemot, or Marleet. If they're out there, it could be over in seconds. I might survive the first attack since I'm wearing this enchanted armor, but the men would quickly catch me and pierce me with an arrow or sword in a place where the armor doesn't cover. The only one who might make it out alive would be Mic. His armor could cause them to look away or lose interest.

There's no movement in the forest, but I can't quite calm myself down. I feel Ellcia step up next to me, and without thinking, I put my arm around her. She doesn't pull away. I'm not sure if I'm doing this to comfort her or me.

"We have to keep moving. Take what you can, and let's go," Rulf orders.

Mic sets to work right away, going through their packs. He seems to ignore just about anything except money and food. I'm disgusted by the thought of robbing the dead, but I know the food might be exactly what we need to survive. If I die, I'd rather my supplies go toward keeping others alive. Somehow, that thought feels like I'm justifying something horrible.

We scramble around and take the food and money. I try not to look at their faces. At one point, I bump into Marleet. Her face is drained of all color, and tears stream down her cheeks. I know her well enough to know that she's not struggling as much with the taking of the food, but just the fact that the men are dead.

When we finish, we move on, but Rulf has us stay low. I find the effort involved in trying to crouch and move with my pack is far greater than normal walking.

We move farther north and reach the edge of the cliff-face, then follow it along to the east. Ten minutes later, I want to scream. Nothing feels right. Everything from the height of the cliffs, the forest filled with trees and bugs, the dead men, the snares and freshly cooked rabbit, the armor, the weapons, the idea that the Regent wants us dead… none of it feels real or right or…

I'm at a loss. I don't know how to take it all.

Rulf calls a halt and sits down on a rock. I decide I want to take charge of something. I want to understand. I'm just so frustrated.

I stand before Rulf and blurt out, "How did you know about the secret passageway?"

Rulf doesn't answer at first. Instead, he just sits there and stares at me. A moment later, he pulls out an apple he found on one of the dead men and bites into it.

I start to feel a little silly. Everyone is staring at me. I realize not only am I asking that question with far more intensity than the question itself calls for, but it seems out of place. I would think I'd be asking any number of questions before that one.

When Rulf finally answers, he simply says, "Grew up in the castle."

I hear someone step up beside me, and I glance over to see Ellcia. She looks just as confused as I feel. On the other side of me, Hemot and Marleet appear. Hemot is partway through what appears to be half a cooked chicken. I'm assuming he found that on the men we just looted.

"But, why aren't you there now? You couldn't have been more than four or five when the rebellion happened. I thought you were younger than me, and I was six."

"I'm two years younger than you, Caric."

Rulf didn't answer my question, and I decide I want to push it. "Why aren't you there now? Or… why weren't you there until we set out to find the Prince?"

"I wanted to be with Mic. He needed me."

I want to ask why, but then I feel like it'll sound like I can't imagine anyone would want to leave the castle to be with someone like Mic. Instead, I just try to push a little more. "We were all kids in the castle when the rebellion happened, and they kept us on. We were given the jobs our parents had."

Rulf growls and stands to his feet. I see Mic off to the side. At the mention of all of us doing our parent's jobs, his head shoots up, and he stares at me in shock.

Rulf takes a step toward me and brandishes the apple at me like it's a weapon. "None of your parents were servants in the castle! None of them cleaned the walls or swept the floors!"

"I take care of curtains!" Hemot says with a smile. The piece of chicken stuck to his chin only adds to the absurdity of his statement.

Rulf growls at Hemot, but then turns back to his rock. He sits down again and attacks the apple like he's angry with it. In another couple mouthfuls, it's gone—core and all.

"You knew our parents?" Ellcia asks.

"I knew all your parents!"

I try to make sense of that. "But… you were only five."

"I was."

I can see he's getting that look in his eye that says the conversation is just about done. I desperately try to plow forward, hoping to get some clarity. I'm not sure I've ever felt so curious in my life. I know nothing about my parents, other than they were servants in the castle. My few memories of them are vague and confusing. I think my dad must have been the head steward, because everyone around him listened to him and did what he said. I think my mom must have been one of the most important servants because she was so well respected by the other women and always wore beautiful dresses. But something about my memories no longer make complete sense to me.

"How do you remember all this?"

Mic speaks up at that point. "Never forgets. Never forgets."

Rulf growls at him but nods his head. "I'm not like other kids. I never forget anything. I was always ahead of the rest of you."

"The rest of us?" Marleet says. "Did we spend time together?"

"We were friends," Rulf growls. "The six of us played together all the time. I used to read you stories."

I laugh at that, but no one else does. "You read us stories?"

"I was reading before I was two years old. Mic's right. I never forget. I can remember each and every story. I can remember everything I've ever read or studied. I remember everything that's ever happened to me. Ever."

"And you said you knew our parents?" Marleet asks.

"Yes. I knew all your parents. My dad served your dad," Rulf says, pointing at me.

"Doing what?" I ask.

Rulf ignores the question and says, "Your name isn't even Caric."

My mouth drops open. All questions just fade from my mind. All I can think of right now is how confused I am. What could he possibly mean?

"Is my name actually Ellcia?" I hear from beside me.

That question pulls me back. As silly as it seems to me, I realize that troubles me more than finding out my own name isn't really Caric. I had always thought her name was beautiful. I don't want her to lose it.

"Yes," Rulf says. "The rest of you have your actual names. My name isn't Rulf, though, not really, and Mic's name's not Mic."

Mic jumps to his feet at that and comes up to Rulf. He punches him in the arm and says, "Private! Private!"

Rulf growls back at Mic, but Mic stands his ground. After a few moments, Rulf says, "Sorry. I shouldn't have said all that." He turns back to us and says, "You all have to keep this to yourselves. Mic doesn't like me talking about him."

"Can you talk about us some more?" Marleet asks.

"Yeah," I say. "We don't know anything about ourselves, other than what we've been told. And I think we've been told a lot of lies. If our parents weren't servants, what were they?"

"Don't any of you remember?" Rulf asks, pulling out what appears to be the other half of the chicken that Hemot had been working on.

We all shake our heads. I see Marleet step up next to Hemot, and she takes his arm, but she backs away with a disgusted look on her face when she sees how aggressively he's going at his half of the chicken.

"Why did someone change my name? And if our parents weren't servants, what were they? And how can you remember everything?" I ask, then add, "And how were you reading at two years of age?"

"Before two. I'm really smart."

I shake my head. I know he's smart, but then he always seems kind of dumb as well.

Hemot laughs and says, "Really? How smart?"

Rulf growls and storms off. I realize we got a lot more out of him this time, but now we have even more questions. My mind drifts back to Hob's comments about me. He referred to me as royalty and to Ellcia as "Lady Ellcia."

I should have realized it when I found out about the assassins, but it's just hit me. It's not just that we're one of the Vanguard. Everything's changed now. The Regent is not the man I thought he was—that's for sure. But the big thing is... we won't be going back to the castle unless the Prince is found. And perhaps not even then.

7

---•---

The Run

We continue through Switcher Pass for the rest of the day, moving slightly south away from the cliff-face once again. When we make camp, Rulf insists we not have a fire. None of us mind. The nights aren't cold, and it just means we'll likely fall asleep earlier. He says he'll light one in the morning if he catches any food.

Once we've set up camp, he has us practice with our actual swords—not sticks. At first, I think that'll be too loud, but he says that we're just trying to get used to them and are not going to practice with one another. We spend an hour or so going through the forms and working on keeping our legs and feet where they should be. We're just swinging our blades through the air, but it's a lot of fun.

The next morning, Rulf checks his snares and finds he didn't catch anything. He mumbles something about Switcher Pass, and we move on.

My feet are still sore, and my muscles hurt a lot, but I find I'm not struggling as much, and my muscles warm up quickly each day. I also notice that the huge bruise on Mic's face is starting to clear up. I'm not sure I've ever seen him without it. He seems to be enjoying himself. I don't talk to him much, though. The few times I've tried to engage him in conversation, it's hard to get anywhere, and he just shuts down.

At around mid-morning, we come across the next Vanguard. They are, like the first, all dead. It appears as though some of them put up a bit of a fight as four of the men have their swords drawn, and one sword even has blood on it, but there's no sign of the assassins. We search the bodies and take their food and money. I wonder why the assassins don't at least rob the men, but then I think about the amount of money we're getting. None of the dead men have much of anything on them. We'll be lucky if we can purchase enough food for one day with what we've collected.

No one asks any questions until we're out of sight of the dead Vanguard. At that point, Ellcia speaks up. "How do you know it's the same men who killed this group?"

Mic is the one who answers. He simply says, "Rulf knows. Rulf knows. Rulf always knows. Rulf always knows."

Rulf gives his traditional growl and then explains, "Thieves move through this area, but they never attack armed men. The Vanguards were killed by professionals, and professionals won't attack unless they're paid to do so. That's two Vanguards gone, at least. There are only four in total."

Ellcia starts to ask another question, but Mic interrupts her by running in front of Rulf. He slams his shoulder into Rulf's belly and whispers. "Back. Back. Turn around. Turn around."

"What's wrong?" Hemot asks.

Mic shakes his head and hisses, "Quiet. Quiet."

Rulf turns and pushes us back. I move through the forest as quickly as I can, and Mic directs us behind a large tree. Once around it, he pulls Rulf slowly out and points. Rulf shakes his head for a moment, but then his mouth drops open. He turns his head back to us, and I see something on Rulf's face that I never would have thought possible.

He appears genuinely afraid.

He glances around as if he's looking for an escape route and doesn't seem to relax until he looks a short distance to the north. I look in that direction, and I can see the ground rise up a bit. It looks to me like there might be a way through that will prevent us from being seen.

"What is it?" I hiss at Rulf.

He shakes his head at me. "Reber Troll."

I glance around at Ellcia. She looks just as confused as I feel. A quick look back at Marleet tells me she's in no better position to tell me anything. I only know of Reber Trolls by name, not much more. Only Hemot looks like he understands. Unfortunately, his expression matches Rulf's.

"Where is it?"

Rulf points, and I move around the edge of the tree. I look through the forest and can't see anything out of the ordinary at first. I ask him to tell me where exactly, and he points toward a large rock. I scan the area again, but still can't make it out. I'm about to ask him one more time when I realize what I'm looking at. What I thought was a large rock is actually the troll.

It's huge!

Its skin is gray and does, in fact, look like stone. The head is broad with wide-set eyes and a mouth that's disturbingly large. The mouth itself is partly open, and I can see a few teeth. They look yellowed with age.

The body and the arms show muscle and fat bulging through saggy, thick-looking skin. The hands have four fingers each, and I assume the feet, which I cannot quite see as they're behind some bushes, have four toes as well. I suspect if the creature stood up, it would be about four times my height.

It hasn't moved one bit, and I'm about to wave the others to come around and see it when I notice the eyes. The eyes are large, about the size of my fists. It blinks now and then, slowly dropping the lids down and raising them up again. The terrifying part, however, is that the eyes are fixed on me.

"Don't move fast, Caric," Rulf says. "Drop your gaze. Don't look at it."

I look down at the forest floor and lower my head for good measure. I hear a deep grunt from the direction of the Reber Troll and hope that it doesn't mean the monster is going to come for us. If it can move fast, there will be little we can do to stop it.

"Everyone follow me," Rulf whispers. "Keep your eyes on the ground. Don't make eye contact with it. Don't make any noises that you don't have to make. If you make a loud noise, don't apologize, don't try to cover it up, just go on walking quietly. Let's do our best to make it out of here alive."

We follow Rulf through the forest, trying hard to walk silently. Living in the city, I have never seen anything like that before, but I'm guessing they're dangerous. I'm not surprised after looking at the thing.

We reach the area where the ground rises up a bit and is covered in large rocks. I have a bit of a panic that it might be more trolls, but a second glance lets me know there's nothing to fear.

We travel along until we're confident we're far enough away, and Rulf and Hemot visibly relax. Rulf drops down on the ground and leans back against a tree. I knew he was scared, but I had no idea it had terrified him that much.

"What's a Reber Troll?" Marleet asks.

Hemot answers with a shake of his head. "It's something we never want to meet—or at least meet again. They're indestructible. A hundred trained soldiers can't take one down. If you're lucky enough to break its skin with a sword or a spear, you only make it angrier."

"Are they fast?" Ellcia asks, looking back over her shoulder.

"No," Rulf says. "Not at all. They walk at about the speed of a fast walk for us. You can outrun it over a short distance with no trouble."

"Then what's the danger?" I ask.

"Never stops. Never stops," Mic says.

Rulf nods. "That's right. It just never stops. If you anger it, it will chase you to the end of the earth. It will move at that steady pace until it catches you. You can't lose it once it settles on your scent. If a Reber Troll is after you, no city will take you in. They'll toss you over the wall to the Reber Troll rather than give you sanctuary."

"Why?" Ellcia asks. "Don't the walls stop it?"

"Even if the walls could stop it, do you think you'd want one of those things patrolling around your city day in and day out for the rest of eternity?"

I'm beginning to understand. It's a terrifying thought.

"But it wouldn't matter, because the walls won't stop it," Rulf says. "A Reber Troll will just slowly tear its way through the wall or gates or whatever barrier you have set up. There's a city on the other side of Switcher Pass that tried to resist a Reber Troll a long time ago. It was one of the strongest, most secure cities in the kingdom at the time. The son of the Lord of the city upset a Reber Troll, and it came after him. He hid in the city, and the Reber Troll entered the city and began to slowly tear down building after building. No one in the city, aside from the man who had upset it, died. They had to leave, though. The city is not much more than rubble now. The Reber Troll tore down every stone wall and every building over a period of four months until there was nothing left. Then it picked up the scent of the

Lord's son and went after him. It took the troll six years, but it eventually caught up to the man and killed him. I've heard of cities that when they see a Reber Troll coming, they just open all the gates and hope the beast will walk in one gate and out the other. If it doesn't, they all prepare to leave. There's nothing else they can do. Nothing can stop a Reber Troll."

I don't like the sound of this. "How do you anger it?"

Rulf shrugs his shoulders. "Don't know."

My mouth drops open. I was beginning to think Rulf knew everything. He knows how to survive in the wild and even set a snare. He knew all about the assassins and knows more about us than I feel like we know about ourselves. He knows all about the Reber Troll... except he doesn't know the one piece of information that could keep us safe from the creature.

"I know," Hemot says.

I look at him in surprise but remember that he was the only one of us who didn't look confused a few minutes ago when the Reber Troll was first mentioned.

We all turn to Hemot, and a big smile grows on his face. He sticks out his chest as if he's proud of himself and says, "It's really easy to upset a Reber Troll. You do it by annoying it. I've read a bit about them. There have been people who have run into the side of one or even a man who accidentally shot an arrow and hit the Reber Troll in the side of the head, but it didn't upset the creature. However, there have been people who have walked too close to it, and the thing goes berserk. Something annoys it, and it comes after you. There are reports of loud noises or talking or laughter that have upset a Reber Troll. If you wake it from its sleep, that annoys it. If you make too much noise or move too fast around it, it's sure to come after you."

"Is it coming after us now?" Marleet asks.

"I think we'd see it or hear it if it was," Hemot says. "The thing I don't understand, though," he says with a frown, "is why the Reber Troll is here. Normally they're only found in the Talic Region and sometimes in the mountains."

Rulf grunts his agreement and pushes himself back onto his feet. "Time to move."

We continue east and then a little north again. Rulf wants to keep us close to the cliff-face. He tells us that since the ground is rockier in this area, we'll be harder to track. The downside is there isn't as much chance for food or water in this terrain.

Until this point, we've had plenty of access to water. I haven't actually given it much thought. Today, however, I notice that my waterskin is just about empty, and there hasn't been a stream for a while. We still have food, but without water, we're in trouble.

As we move, Rulf and Mic keep whispering back and forth. I really don't understand those two. They seem like a really unusual pair. I realize that I've never asked if Mic grew up in the castle, although Rulf suggested that he did. But then, it doesn't make sense to me that two kids would leave the castle on their own at ages five and six. Why wouldn't they just stay with the rest of us?

My mind drifts back to the rebellion. Rulf didn't say what my dad did. I was told he was a servant, but I don't remember that kind of thing. I remember him dressed in fancy clothes. I remember him wearing armor. The armor he wore, even though I was so young, had looked quite impressive to me. I remember everyone obeyed him… but even a head steward doesn't wear armor, fancy clothes, and order everyone around.

My mom was in charge as well. No one questioned her. She was tall and strong and… dangerous. She was never dangerous to me, but I knew others feared and respected her.

Just as I start to think again about my memories of the throne room and Hob calling me "Your Highness", I push the thoughts down. I don't even want to consider it anymore. It all... scares me.

I glance over at Ellcia... or as Hob called her, Lady Ellcia. I wonder to myself who she really was. I'm sure she and Marleet and Hemot are all wondering the same kinds of things about themselves. I really want to know who I am, but at the same time I kind of wish I was still at the castle, polishing statues and cleaning floors.

I'm distracted from my thoughts as I notice two things. First, Rulf and Mic keep glancing behind us. Second, we've picked up speed. We're nearly at a run, and I'm already breathing quite hard.

Rulf hisses, "Follow close behind me. Do exactly what I do!"

He turns quickly to the left just as a loud thud sounds near my head. I glance back to see a crossbow bolt lodged deep in a tree.

We break into an all-out run, moving our way back and forth through the trees. Hemot, with his long legs, is right behind Rulf and Mic. Ellcia starts to trail behind after a few minutes. I notice Marleet has slipped right to the back. I let Ellcia get in front of me and slip behind Marleet. Her face is flushed, and she looks terrified.

I tell her to keep running and slow down just enough to run directly behind her. Before I realize what I've done, I've set myself up as a shield for her. The moment I do realize it, however, I immediately go through a range of emotions from courage to terror to compassion for Marleet to embarrassment at doing the most absurd thing I can imagine doing to humiliation at the thought that I'd rather someone else be the shield.

I have that armor that's impenetrable. I guess I'm the best one to do this. I hope it can actually stop a crossbow.

Rulf weaves us back and forth, and a few more bolts end up whizzing past us or lodging into trees. One bolt hits a large rock and ricochets off to the left, narrowly missing Hemot.

The cliff-face is still to our left, and we're drawing right up next to it. What's strange, however, is the ground is rising on the right as well. Before long, the rocks and small hills on the right have turned into another cliff, albeit a small one compared to the one on the left. I can see through the thinning trees ahead that the cliffs are coming close together. I fear they'll meet, and we'll reach a dead-end. If so, our pursuers will easily kill us off.

I holler out to Rulf, "The rocks on the right…"

"I know!" he growls back. "We can't stop!"

The air is forced out of my lungs, and I crash onto the ground, rolling for a few feet before I slam into a tree. I can't breathe, and my back and shoulders ache. I'm not sure what's happened at first, but then I get it. I've been hit in the back with a crossbow bolt. The pain from the bolt shoots through me before I remember to concentrate. I know it hasn't penetrated my body, so it can't actually hurt me. But real or not, I can't get the air back into my lungs, and I'm starting to panic.

When the men rush up, I'm not moving. They ignore me, not offering much more than a glance at what likely appears to be the body of a recently killed teenage boy.

I stretch and twist and suddenly find I can take a deep breath. I try to be as quiet as I can, but I don't think I was successful. Pushing myself to my feet, I draw my sword. My friends might need my help.

I rush through the forest. Most of the ground is covered in a thick, soft dirt or pine needles which makes little sound as I run. Ahead, I can see the assassins. A quick count looks like there's nine.

When I reach them, I stay just out of sight behind a large tree. My friends have their backs to a rock wall. The two cliffs did end up meeting, and there's no way out. Ellcia, Hemot, and Marleet look terrified, and each one seems to be pushing the others behind themselves in an attempt to protect one another. Mic stands by himself, mumbling over and over, "Don't hurt us. Don't hurt us."

Rulf, however, is nowhere to be seen. I wonder if he was shot like me, but without the armor, he'd be dead.

"Ah, here we are, then," one of the assassins calls out. Each man holds a crossbow in his arms, but not one points it at my friends. There's no real need. They have nowhere to run. "You are the last Vanguard," the one man continues. "I will admit, I didn't think you would be the hardest of the four groups to kill. The others didn't seem to even know we were coming, but you have all managed to evade us." He laughs and then adds, "Until now."

8

The Assassins

I want to run out and rescue my friends, but I'm absolutely terrified. I'm not sure what I'm supposed to do or when the best time is to attack. I wish I could communicate with the others.

"Weren't there six of them?" one of the other men asks. "The one's down, but there's supposed to be a really big guy."

The man who seems to be in charge pauses for a moment before saying, "We'll have a good look for him once we're done here."

"And weren't there twelve of you?" Hemot asks defiantly.

The one in charge laughs again, and I recognize him as Searle, the man who spoke to the Regent. Any hope that maybe the Regent might be my friend is gone. "We always lose some along the way. That means when it comes time to divide the money, there's more to go around. One of the Vanguard put up a bit of a fight, and we lost a young guy who really hadn't been much help anyway. The other two have stayed back in case any of you escape our grasp. They'll pick you off easily."

I grip my sword tightly and prepare myself to charge. I hope my armor will keep me alive long enough to rescue my friends, but then I fear it might just keep me from dying. It won't stop me from losing a hand or a leg.

I close my eyes for a second and take a deep breath. I'm about to scream and charge when Rulf beats me to it, charging out of the forest to my left. He attacks two men right away. I hear what sounds like sticks breaking, but I'm sure that's the bones of the two men Rulf is twisting in his hands with his inhuman strength.

Now's the time. I charge forward just as my friends charge as well. I use my sword on the first man I reach. I don't want to kill him, so I don't drive the sword right into him. Instead, I slash the sword against the thick part of his armor at his shoulders, hoping to injure him with the impact rather than actually harm him. But when my sword strikes the man, I'm shocked to see that it not only slices right through the armor, but through the entire man's back and down to his hip. I watch in horror as the man falls in two pieces to the ground.

Another man charges me with his sword drawn. Without thinking, I swing my sword. He easily raises his own up to deflect the blow, but instead of deflecting my swing, his sword is sliced in two, and I feel very little resistance as my blade continues through the man's armor and through his chest.

I turn back to the others, trying my best to focus. I know we have to do what we can to survive. Ellcia and Marleet are wrestling a man to the ground, although it doesn't look like they'll hold him down much longer. Hemot has managed to pin down one of the men. Another of the assassins is on the ground with a bolt through his neck, which I assume was Mic's doing. Still another man lays at Mic's feet, and Mic is battling it out like a madman with yet another of the men, swords flashing back and forth. That man goes down a second later. Mic is good with the sword, but I expect the armor is making it difficult for the assassins to concentrate on him.

I want to go help the others, but I'm afraid my sword will just as easily cut through my friends as it will through the men. I find myself rooted to the ground, unsure of what to do.

Mic runs up to the assassin Hemot is fighting and finishes the man off quickly with his sword. I glance back at Ellcia and Marleet, just as the man throws them off. They land with a thud, and he draws his sword. Before he can attack, however, Rulf reaches him.

The man's sword clatters to the ground as his body is lifted into the air. The look on Rulf's face is a look of rage and hunger, and I watch in revulsion as Rulf attacks. I find myself at a loss for how to understand what I'm seeing, other than to say that Rulf… breaks the man.

I turn around and quickly count the bodies, keeping my eyes from landing on the ones I killed. All nine are accounted for.

I feel arms wrap around me, and it's Hemot. A moment later, Ellcia and Marleet join him.

"We thought you were dead!" Hemot says, his voice choking up.

"Yeah, well," I say, "I learned something new. Apparently, my armor can stop a crossbow bolt."

When they let me go, Rulf and Mic are standing over the two bodies of the assassins—the ones in pieces. I do my best to avoid looking at the mess. I have, obviously, never killed a man, let alone in such a brutal way.

Rulf grunts at me and says, "Let me see your sword."

I glance down at it. I'm shocked that it's entirely clean. I'm not sure I want to give it up to him, but I also want to get rid of it. It seems like not only my greatest treasure but also an evil that should be buried deep in the earth and never used again.

I hand it over, and Rulf examines it. Mic steps up close and whispers, "Good sword. Good sword."

Rulf walks back a few steps toward a small tree, swings it lightly at the trunk, and the sword slices clean through. The tree topples to the ground, and Rulf examines the blade again. He then steps up next to a large rock, sets the tip of the blade on the rock and drives it directly in, sinking it up to the hilt.

We all gasp. The blade is, like my armor, enchanted.

Rulf gives it a light tug, and the blade slides out again. He growls something under his breath and hands it back.

I look at the blade again, and I see there's not even a scratch on the blade, nor is there any indication it has ever seen battle. I decide to put it back into its sheath, but then wonder how it is that it doesn't cut its way out and then fall to the ground. I imagine it sinking into the dirt, and I wonder how deep it'll go before it stops. I push the thoughts away and figure the sheath must be enchanted as well as the sword.

I shake my head and turn back to the others. They're looking at me and my sword in wonder.

"No time to worry about enchanted blades," Rulf says. "We have to get past the other two men. If they're hiding in the trees, we won't see them until the arrows are sunk into our chests."

I turn back to the rock wall ahead of us. The two cliffs have come together to form a dead-end, but I wonder if we can climb it. There's no doubt the surviving assassins will have placed themselves in a spot where they can easily see anyone coming back. I wonder to myself if we can use the armor from the men we killed to disguise ourselves, but one false move will give us away.

Mic points at the rocks ahead in his awkward manner. "One way. One way."

Rulf nods. "Mic's right. We can't go back. The men they have hidden in the trees will get all of you."

"Not you?" Hemot asks.

Rulf grunts and says, "Not me." Turning to face us all, he says, "Pull out your knives and swords. See if any of the rest of them will cut into rock."

We all check our daggers and our swords, but none of them are enchanted in that way, although I wonder what other enchantments we might find. I also briefly wonder who might have enchanted the blade. Spellcasters are rare. I don't even know if there are any known Spellcasters living at this time. And what's scariest of all is knowing that they're rarely good.

Rulf tells me he needs my sword, and I hand it over again. I'm afraid this time he won't give it back. At first, I thought I wanted nothing to do with it, but now I'm thinking of how great it is to have a blade like that.

He rushes to the cliff ahead of us. To the left is the cliff face that borders Switcher Pass. It's about two or maybe three times the height of the tallest walls at the castle. On the right, and in front of us, where the other smaller cliff joins up to the large one, the cliff is only about the height of a two-story building.

"Listen!" Rulf barks. "I'm going to climb the cliff. While I climb, search the bodies for food or money." He then turns back to the cliff, pulls out his dagger, and climbs. I know I'm supposed to be searching the bodies, but at first, I'm fascinated with watching him. He drives my sword with his right hand into the side of the cliff, flat of the blade downwards, and uses it to boost himself up, pulling himself up by his right arm. Once he's holding his entire weight with the one arm, he uses his own dagger and his feet to find cracks and crevices to support himself. When he's secure, he pulls my sword out of the rock, reaches up higher, drives it into the rock again, and pulls himself up with his right arm.

I glance over at the others, and they're just as enthralled as I am. However, I remember the two men behind us, waiting to kill us. If they grow impatient, they could come after us at any moment.

"Let's go!" I order. We all search the bodies. I feel a little sick about doing this, but not as bad as I did the first two times. As I look through packs and pockets, I remember Searle had said we were the last Vanguard. That must mean they found the third one and killed them as well. It hits me that the two assassins behind us are not going to be pleased. When they find out their friends are dead, they're going to come after us with a vengeance.

"Hey!" growls Rulf. "Time to move." He tosses down a rope with a loop on the bottom and says, "Mic, you first."

"No. No," Mic says. He grabs Marleet and pushes her forward. Marleet doesn't look like she wants to go first, but she puts her foot in the loop. She grabs hold of the rope, and Rulf heaves her up with little difficulty. He then lowers the rope for Mic, but he refuses again and passes the rope on to Hemot. Next goes Ellcia, then Mic pushes me forward. "Go. Go," Mic says.

I shake my head. I don't know much about what's honorable or not honorable, but I'm confident it's wrong to leave a boy like Mic down here by himself. I shove the rope into his hands and holler, "Go!" with as much authority as I can.

Mic nods and slips his foot into the loop. A few seconds later, he's out of sight. The rope drops down right by me, and I put my foot into the loop and grab hold. I holler up, "Ready!" just as I catch a glimpse of a man standing in the forest a short distance away. I hear the snap of the crossbow release and feel the bolt slam into my chest just at my heart.

The force of the bolt knocks me back against the rock, and I scream. I concentrate hard to believe that the bolt hasn't entered me, and the pain slowly slips away. I see the man run off to the side as a crossbow bolt sinks into the trunk of a tree near where he stood. Mic must be returning fire. An arrow flies through the air as well, but it hits nowhere near the man. Hemot must be trying to shoot the guy with his bow. I grab the rope and holler up again, and Rulf heaves me up far faster than any of the others. I see one of the men take aim and fire at someone above me, and I holler, "Get down," but I don't know if it helps. All I know is Rulf continues to pull on the rope.

When I get to the top, he yanks me out of sight of the men below, and I see Mic laying on the edge with his crossbow aimed down into the forest. The others crouch back a short distance from the edge. Rulf pushes me along, and we scramble down a rock slope leading back down to the forest ahead of us. As we run, Rulf slows me down and hands me my sword. I quickly put it into the sheath, and we run.

I don't know if the men will try to climb the cliff or make their way around. Either way, we don't have much time.

We run down the rest of the decline until we reach the forest, but Rulf keeps us close to the cliff on the north side. The ground is all rock here, and I think he wants us not to leave tracks.

I'm not actually sure that's all that helpful. If we went through the forest, we'd leave tracks. If we don't leave any tracks, then they'll know we're running along the rocks. I don't say anything, though. Rulf usually knows what he's doing.

We continue along the rocks, running as fast as we can. I'm glad I'm not struggling as much as I did at first. The others seem to be doing a lot better as well. It looks like we're getting pretty used to traveling—or running—although my feet still ache constantly.

After a long time, Rulf slows down and comes to a stop. He turns around and runs back a short way before waving us over. "This way!" he hollers, and runs into the forest.

I rush to where he stood before he took off into the trees and see he's taken a well-worn path. The newly found path is not very wide, and we'll have to travel single file, but it looks like a good option. The ground is hard-packed dirt, and the bushes and plants are growing far enough from the path that we shouldn't leave any signs that we traveled this way. As I run down the path with Mic, Ellcia, and Marleet ahead of me and Hemot behind me, I realize that even if we do leave signs, the path is obviously used enough that there would be little chance of figuring out if we are the ones who have left the tracks or if they came from someone else.

Despite how much better I'm doing with the traveling, my legs grow tired. The girls ahead of me are slowing down. I feel like I have a little more in me, but not enough to encourage them to pick up the speed. Ellcia calls up to Rulf to get him to slow down. He comes to a stop, and we halt.

"We can't stop here. They'll catch us," he says.

"We can't keep running," Ellcia says between gasps. "We have to find a way to lose the assassins."

Rulf turns every direction, and I can see him searching the forest for signs of pursuit. I think maybe he's also looking for another option. I can't think of anything other than running, but I'm hoping he'll come up with something.

"There's a village not far from here," he finally says. "That might mean there are more paths, and it'll be easier to hide our tracks. We might lose the assassins at the village, but we'll have to keep going."

Ellcia nods her head, and Rulf runs on. I'm grateful that he's moving a little slower. I'm not sure it matters much, though. A little slower isn't enough. We all need to stop. We just have no choice but to keep going.

Our first sign that there's a village nearby comes when we pass a man walking through the woods carrying some rabbits he captured. He waves at us, but that's all. We continue without stopping as the man whistles a tuneless song.

It seems so strange and out of place to see someone just going about their normal life. It feels like everything has changed, and everyone should be on alert for danger.

Our second sign of a village is when we pass four children running along the path. When they see us, their eyes fill with terror, and they take off through the trees and bushes. I want to run after them to tell them that we won't hurt them, but chasing them will probably only make it worse. Besides, I realize they might be helping us. If the two assassins are still tracking us, they might see signs of people running through the bushes, and it might take them a bit to figure out it wasn't us. Then my heart fills with terror at the thought of the men killing the children, but I push that out of my head. These are men hired to do a job. They won't kill anyone they're not paid to kill. I hope.

We reach the edge of the village, and Rulf leads us right into it. Wood and stone houses, most with thatched roofs, are built around the area in what looks like an almost random order. Th villagers within sight stare at us in a guarded manner as if we are either an intrusion or a threat, but no one calls out to us. When we reach the center of the village, we turn east and run the rest of the way past all the houses. The people look relieved to see we aren't slowing down.

When we get to the far side of the village, Rulf finds a path moving through the forest and takes it. By this point, I'm finding it hard to get my feet off the ground. With each step, I wonder if the next one will be my last. But the others manage, so I push on.

My pack feels like it's getting heavier by the second. I stumble off to the side just a bit and nearly fall into the bushes but pull myself back again. Ellcia glances at me, and I see terror mixed with the exhaustion. It was hard enough to face off against the assassins, but to think they could be hiding in amongst the trees or coming up on us at this very moment is a lot to handle.

A few paths move off to the north and to the south, but Rulf ignores them. When he finds one that he likes heading south, we move in that direction.

We run on and on until Rulf finally slows down. The path starts veering to the east again, but Rulf pushes through the bushes and leads us at a slow pace deeper south. I had thought we weren't supposed to leave a trail behind us with things like breaking through bushes, but I'm hoping Rulf remembers that. Mic seems to think he never forgets anything.

About an hour later, Rulf stops, drops his pack on the ground, and settles down against a tree. The rest of us collapse, and I just pull off my pack and lie down on the ground. Someone's pack rolls up against me, but I just ignore it. I find I can't sleep, but it feels good to just stop moving for a bit. I hear a snore beside me and open my eyes. It's Hemot. He's out cold.

I lay there for a long time. Rulf grunts, and it sounds like he's getting up and moving off into the trees. The time passes slowly for me, but eventually I drift off.

9

Out of Switcher Pass

When I wake, Rulf's sitting over a fire. He's cooking a small rabbit that appears to have just been caught. From the light, I'm guessing it's early evening. My mind's a little slow, but I think that means I've only slept for an hour or two.

I pull myself up. I don't like the way I feel, but my body tells me I'm not going to sleep any longer. The others are all still out. Hemot lies on his back in a weird position, sprawled over his pack, and he's snoring like there's something seriously wrong with his throat. I feel sorry for him and try to push him into a better position, but in his sleep, he fights me off bravely. I leave him to his misery and drop down next to Rulf at the fire.

A moment later, Ellcia wakes up and sits down beside me. Rulf doesn't say anything to us. Instead, he just focuses on the rabbit. I'm guessing he has multiple snares set up, but he must have caught one quickly. I'm glad. It smells great, and I can't wait to dig in.

Ellcia and I chat for a little while, but I find she's not really in a talking mood. I am, so I turn to Rulf. He's a hard one to get information out of, but I've settled into the idea that I can learn bits and pieces here and there.

"Thanks, Rulf," I say.

He looks surprised for a moment, then asks, "For what?"

"For all you're doing. We wouldn't be alive today if you weren't with us. None of us knew how to hunt or fight or to watch out for the assassins."

Rulf grunts a reply. When I look at him, I have to remind myself that he's a smart guy. Nothing about his appearance comes across as anything more than a brute.

I decide to dive into some of the topics we're all quite curious about. Hemot, Marleet, and Mic all appear sound asleep. Maybe it's a good time just to focus in and chat. "Hey Rulf, why does the Regent want us dead?" It feels good to ask that question. Until recently, I had been really holding onto the hope that the Regent really isn't a bad person.

Rulf turns the rabbit on the spit a little more and then asks, "What do you know about the rebellion?"

"We studied it a lot in school. The Airite tribe wanted the throne. There had been a king from the Airites nearly a millennium ago, and they wanted the throne back. No one suspected them as they were considered a peaceful tribe and citizens of Sevord. Once enough of them were in the city, they attacked the castle, killed the King, and would have held the throne if it were not for the Nobles. The soldiers moved in under Lord Parthun's command and killed the rebels, taking back the throne. He took on the role of Regent as there was a rumor that the Prince survived. The Prince was right around our age at the time. Hard to know where he'd be now."

As I spell all that out, I'm filled with doubt. The Regent has not proved to be as honorable as I thought he was—perhaps much about that story isn't accurate.

"No," Rulf says.

I wait for more, but nothing else seems to be forthcoming. "No, what?"

"No," Rulf says. "The Regent was behind it all."

I shake my head. I'm pretty sure I believe him, but I just find myself struggling to accept what he's saying.

"Can you tell us more?" Ellcia asks quietly. "Tell us what actually happened. And tell us about who we really are."

"I can't tell you who you really are," Rulf says. "The Captain told me not to."

Anger builds in my chest. The Captain has always been against me. He's known all along who I really am, and yet he's kept it from me and is trying to keep Rulf from telling me.

"You don't have to listen to the Captain."

"Yes," Rulf says, "I do. He's one of the few soldiers in the castle loyal to the throne. I'd listen to him even if it cost me my life."

I wasn't quite expecting that level of loyalty from Rulf, nor am I prepared to know how to respond to it. Instead, I decide to let that one go. "Can you at least tell us what really happened during the rebellion?" I notice the forest is a little quieter, and I glance at Hemot. He's awake and has his eyes on us, listening intently. Marleet's on the ground not too far from him, also awake and listening, and Mic has propped himself up against a tree.

Rulf grunts at me but nods his head. I'm hopeful we can actually learn something. "The Airites are the nomads who live in the Talic Region—not many of them left anymore. Parthun hunted a lot of them down years ago. Before the King was killed, they were upset about trade routes going through some of their areas because the new traders were disturbing their flocks, while the traders the nomads relied on were being veered away from their area. The Airites rely on the right kind of trade of wool and corn and more." Rulf grunts again, and I fear that he's about to stop, but he continues. "The Regent, as a Noble and part of the Royal family, oversaw trade for the kingdom. It's suspected he arranged the conflict and then encouraged the Airites to meet with the King... but I don't know any of that for sure. When the Airites arrived, I was in the secret tunnels. I spent a lot of time in there once I found them. I used to listen in on meetings. I watched the meeting with the Airites and the King. The Airites were angry, but they were seeking help. The King had been negotiating with them when he received word of riots in the streets. Before he could act, soldiers rushed in and started killing people. The King fought back with the Airites by his side, but they had no chance. Only the king and a few of the Airites were spared until Parthun arrived."

"What happened?" I asked, my voice barely audible. I glance around at my friends, and they look as horrified as I feel.

"Parthun came in and killed the King."

I remain silent for a moment. I know it's true, but I find myself slipping back into denial. Ellcia speaks up and asks, "Are you sure?"

"I was there. I was sitting inside the secret chamber where we came through into the throne room." He pauses for a moment, then looks straight into Ellcia's eyes. "I watched it happen."

I look around at my friends. Marleet's crying. Hemot looks angry. And Ellcia... the look in Ellcia's eyes tells me her whole world has just come crashing down.

Rulf pulls me back by saying, "I was sneaking through the castle when the Captain found me. He pulled me into a small closet and told me to get out of the castle and go to an abandoned shop near the cobbler who works just outside the eastern gate of the keep. I was to wait there. He told me he was going to try to get others out of the castle—I think you three were some of the ones he was after. As I rushed out of the castle, I found Mic alone in the streets in the midst of the riots. His parents were both dead. My parents were gone. I took him to the abandoned shop, and we waited. No one came for two days. Finally, the Captain arrived with food and water. He told me everything had changed, and that he couldn't get anyone else out. He said the only thing he could do was to try to keep us alive. He's funneled food, water, and supplies out of the castle to us for over ten years."

My mind spins, but at the same time, I decide to push back. "But he was really rough with you. He acted like he didn't like you."

Rulf nods and gives a grunt. "That's our agreement. If we're ever seen together, he treats me roughly. I'm supposed to just take it and act like I'm scared of him. He used the opportunity this time to give me instructions."

"Can you tell us anything about ourselves?" Marleet asks, speaking up for the first time since we started the conversation.

Rulf pauses for a moment and stares into the fire. He adjusts the rabbit a bit, and I think it might be just about done. Finally, he says, "I can tell you that each of you are either royalty or children of high-ranking Nobles."

I hear a gasp from Hemot and Marleet. I glance over at Ellcia, and she doesn't look surprised. That little comment from Hob must have been swimming around in her head.

I feel sick to my stomach. It doesn't make sense to me, and yet it does. I end up asking, "If that's true, then why would the Regent keep us around and keep us as servants? He even told me over and over that he was so glad he rescued us."

"Rescued you!" Hemot said. "He always made it clear that he was so glad he rescued you, Caric! He never said that to me."

"Or me," Marleet said.

I glance at Ellcia, and she shakes her head.

I frown and feel a little guilty. I had tried to leave out that specific point, but it's true. He seemed pleased to have "rescued" all of us, but especially me.

"It's because you're his favorite," Rulf says. "The Captain said the Regent made you and the others his servants because he thinks it's funny that the children of the kingdom's greatest leaders and royals serve him as cleaning and kitchen staff. He wants to declare to anyone who knows what's going on or to any of your parents if they're still alive, 'Look! I've turned your children into servants. They serve me, the one who drove you out!' He thinks it's all a good joke."

"Then why am I his favorite?" I ask.

Rulf growls at me. "I told you I can't tell you!"

"Then does the Regent want to find the Prince?" Marleet asks.

Rulf shakes his head. "Not in the way you thought. If the Prince is found and people recognize him, Parthun will kill him. This isn't the first time he's sent out search parties into the countryside to find the Prince. The people demand it now and then, and he gives them what they want. But the reason he's sealed up the city and no one can leave without permission is because he's always believed the Prince remained within the walls. He didn't want him slipping out."

I relax a little. It sounds kind of like the Regent doesn't know who the Prince is or exactly where he's been all these years. I had started to think I was the Prince and just didn't know it. I almost laugh out loud at the absurdity of it, but I catch myself. I think back to Hob's comment about me and realize he must have just been saying crazy things. I think as well about my memory of being in the throne room and how my dad was in charge of a lot of people… none of that's really evidence of anything. Maybe my dad was a Lord or Duke or maybe a soldier. But doubt remains as I realize that nothing Rulf said really suggested that I'm not the Prince. Maybe that's why the Regent sees me as his favorite. Maybe he really enjoys the thought that the Prince serves him.

"Did you say some of our parents might still be alive?" Hemot asks.

"Who knows?" Rulf replies. "The army was outside the city at the time and some of the Nobles were away. I think the rebellion was planned for when many of the influential and powerful people were gone. It may be that some of your parents escaped." He shakes his head. "However, you have to remember something. If you were still at the castle, at least one of your parents was likely there as well. Both my parents were there when the Regent made his move."

There's silence for a moment. None of us dare to speak at first, but then Marleet gets up and walks over to Rulf. She wraps her arms around his neck and says, "I'm sorry, Rulf."

The look on Rulf's face is confusion mixed with terror. I see him glance over at Mic for support. Mic just shrugs his shoulders and says, "That girl nice. That girl nice."

I see Ellcia squirm beside me, and I hear her mumble under her breath, "I'm nice too. I just didn't want to hug him, that's all. But I'm a nice person."

I'm not sure what to do with all that, so I just let it go. Instead, I ask, "So, why is the Regent trying to kill us off?"

Marleet still has her arms around Rulf. He looks like he wants to run, and I see him glance off into the forest once or twice. At one point, he moves his hands to push her away, but stops like he's not sure if he should touch her. Finally, she lets go, and he relaxes.

He focuses in on answering my question about the Regent killing us as if it will make the memory of the hug go away, but continues to eye Marleet warily. "Well, now that you're out of his control, the Regent would rather you be dead than get out of the city. As for the Vanguards, he wants to secretly kill them off so he can tell the people that he doesn't want to risk sending out any more search parties. However, if we escape the assassins and succeed in finding the Prince, then he'll just know where the Prince is, and he'll arrange an accident. One of the reasons the Captain put me with all of you is to make sure you survive." Rulf stands up and pulls the rabbit off the fire. He says, "I don't want to talk about this anymore tonight. Let's eat."

"Wait," Hemot says. "I have one more question. Are we safe here? I don't understand why you led us through the village. They'll all know where we are, and they'll tell the assassins."

Rulf grunts at Hemot. "The assassins won't talk to the villagers. They'll try to stay out of sight. I went through the village so our tracks would be hard to follow. They won't know which way through the village we went. We should be safe here for the night."

We settle in for our meal of freshly cooked rabbit and some of the cheese and dry bread that we still have left. Our food supply is starting to get low, and I hope Rulf can catch some more rabbits soon.

That night, I find I fall asleep quickly. It's been an exhausting day.

The next morning, Rulf is, as usual, already awake when I open my eyes. As I pull myself up and pack up my supplies in preparation for another full day, I begin to think that I've never actually seen Rulf sleep. He's always still up when I fall asleep and by the time I get up, he's always been awake long enough to check his snares, clean his catch, and start cooking it.

Once again, he has his night's catch over the fire. He caught two large rabbits, a squirrel, and… something else. Whatever it is, it looks meaty. I hope it's not skunk.

I go around and wake everyone else. I'm typically the first one awake every morning, aside from Rulf. My legs are stiff, so it's kind of hard to bend down to shake everyone awake, but I want to wake them gently, so I take my time.

When we're all up, we settle in for a solid breakfast. The fire's dying out, and we're just about done when Rulf stands up quickly.

"What is it?" I ask. "Do you hear the assassins?"

"No!" he barks. "Everyone, grab your packs now!"

We strap on our packs, and I eye the last of the food. It's not been collected, and I hate to leave it behind. I make sure my sword is secured to my side along with my dagger and see that everyone else is ready.

I'm just about to mention the food when I hear them. In the distance, the sound of men's shouts mixed with savage barking. I'm about to wonder if it's a hunting party, when what looks like thirty or forty men come into view. They're carrying sticks, rakes, hoes, clubs, and more. One of the men points at us and screams, "Murderers!"

"Run!" Rulf orders, and we take off toward the east. As we pass the fire, I see Hemot grab the last of the food still on a spit, and he takes a bite out of the side of it as we move.

My legs instantly feel exhausted, and they still ache from yesterday. After a few minutes of running, however, they seem to settle down and don't hurt as much, leaving me feeling less tired than I did at first.

"Why are they chasing us?" Marleet calls out.

"Don't know," Rulf replies. "Do you want to stop and ask them?"

It hits me what's going on. "It's the assassins!"

"No, it's not," Rulf says. "There's like fifty of them. It's the villagers."

"No, I mean, the assassins have done this! That man called us a murderer. I think the assassins killed someone, and the villagers are assuming it was the people who ran through their village yesterday."

I realize I don't have any proof of that, but it seems to make sense to me. Either that or there are some murderers in the area, and we're just in the wrong place at the wrong time.

"Doesn't matter!" Hemot says. "I think I'm more concerned with not being caught by them than I am with why they are chasing us."

"It's not the men I'm worried about," Marleet says as she speeds up.

I look back over my shoulder, and I find a new burst of energy floods through my body. "Run faster!" I scream.

The men have released the dogs, and the animals rush through the forest toward us. There's not much we can do to slow them down. I want to tell Mic to shoot them, but if he stops, they'll be on him in a second.

Rulf growls really loud and orders, "Keep running! I'll deal with the dogs!"

I don't want to leave Rulf to face the dogs alone, but something about his tone sounds more irritated than sacrificial. He seems to have a way to get through everything.

I keep running as Rulf turns back. I'm scared enough that everything in me wants to outrun all my friends. I'm actually the tallest of all the others, aside from Rulf, and I don't think I'd have any trouble outrunning any one of them over a short distance. It takes all my courage just to keep pace with them. I can't believe I'm letting my fear do this to me.

Behind me, I hear a change in the intensity of the dog's barking. They must have reached Rulf. He's hollering, but he doesn't sound hurt. A moment later, the dog's barking changes to yelps and cries of pain. I dare not look back. I don't like dogs, especially ones that are trying to eat me, but I really don't want to see what Rulf is doing to them to cause them to make that sound.

After a moment, I hear loud crashing through the trees behind me, and Rulf rushes past me and takes his spot in the front of the group as we continue to run. I nearly scream at him. All this time when we've been running from everything, he's just jogging along like he has no concern in the world!

I glance back to see the men still chasing us. They haven't fallen behind all that much, but I think we're slowly getting away from them. The fact that they're without dogs now makes the whole situation a lot better.

We crash through the woods until we find a path. With all the turns we've made, going around trees and rocks and more, I'm no longer sure which direction we're heading. The trees in this area are far too thick for me to look up and see the cliffs to get my bearings.

Rulf leads us to the right, and we follow the path as it winds along. I can't help but notice that if we weren't constantly running for our lives, I would enjoy a walk along this path. A few minutes later, we run across a small bridge that leads over a nice clear brook. It would be peaceful and beautiful, if it were not for the unceasing danger and imminent death with every step.

The only good news is that each one of these chases seems to make us stronger. I can tell that I have far more endurance than even yesterday's experience of fleeing from certain death.

Eventually, we notice the villagers lag behind just a bit more. We use the opportunity to slow down, and I feel like we can maintain this speed for much longer. The path curves to the left and then meets up with a large road that runs right and left from our current path. The new road is well maintained and quite wide. Rulf turns right, and I notice the forest comes to an end a short distance ahead.

When the men behind us reach the main road, one of them yells, "Hurry," and a quick glance behind lets me know they've picked up speed. We push ourselves harder, and in a moment, we leave the forest and enter a large open area. The cliffs break off on either side, heading north and south, and I can't help but think this must be the Talic Region. I had heard that this area is hilly and covered in thick grass and few trees—and that's exactly what's before me. I can't see any people just yet, but I know there are plenty of villages and four large cities.

We rush out into this new region and follow the road as it leads east. There's little opportunity to find hiding spots in the Talic Region. I hope our pursuers give up soon.

"Why did you lead us out here?" Hemot asks between gasps for air. "They'll follow us with no trouble."

Rulf replies with a steady voice. It sounds like he's not even breathing heavy. "I don't think they'll follow us much farther. The Talic Region is too dangerous. Most of the villagers from Switcher Pass don't dare enter it."

"What?" Marleet asks. "Then why would WE enter it?"

"We have to go through it to get to Morgin City," Rulf says. "That's where our papers say we're supposed to go."

I look back over my shoulder and then come to a halt. The men have completely stopped at the edge of the forest. Not one takes a single step further at first, but then one does move forward. As soon as he does, two of the men near him grab his shoulders and yank him back. They then turn and disappear into Switcher Pass, leaving us to go our way.

The whole thing leaves me with the impression that the Talic Region is not going to be any better for us than Switcher Pass.

Maybe this is all a big mistake.

10

The Troll

We continue through the rest of the morning and into the early afternoon. I find I'm much thirstier out in the open than I was in the forest, as the sun beats down on our shoulders and the tops of our heads. It's not long before I'm just about out of water.

In its own way, the area is beautiful. It's hilly and windy, yet peaceful and calm. We haven't seen much wildlife, but Rulf assures us it's all through the area. It'll be harder to set up snares, however, without trees.

The trees that are in the Talic Region are in small forests here and there. They seem to just spring up out of nowhere, but the patches of trees aren't that big. Rulf says we'll try to camp in one at nighttime. He says it'll be safer.

One of the things that I find amazing about the area is how far I can see. When we reach the top of a rise, I can see for miles in every direction, with the exception of back toward Switcher Pass. The cliffs and the forest block my view in that direction.

Ahead of us, to the east, tall mountains rise out of the earth. They're a strange green color and many are snowcapped. I had heard that mountains often have snow on the tops of them, but it's something else to see it in person. Every time I look at them, I want to just stop and stare with my mouth hanging open.

Rulf interrupts my thoughts by bringing us to a stop. "All right, everyone," he says with a growl. "We're well into the Talic Region now, and it's about to get dangerous."

"No," Marleet replies, giving a serious shake of her head.

Rulf remains silent for a moment, then finally asks, "What do you mean, 'no'?"

"I mean NO!" Marleet hollers. "It's already been far too dangerous. It's not okay for anything to get more dangerous."

Rulf stares at her with a look of shock. "It hasn't been dangerous at all. We just had a run-in with some assassins and were chased by angry villagers. Aside from that, it's been easy."

Marleet's voice gets really quiet and comes out shaky as she asks, "What's coming next?"

"Well, where do I start?" Rulf begins. "You've got Reber Trolls, of course. We saw one back in the Pass, but that's unusual. They live out here in the Talic Region in caves and holes in the ground or in ruins of cities they've destroyed. On top of that, you have the Talic Wolves. They're a real problem."

I haven't heard of Talic Wolves, aside from Captain Tilbur mentioning them, although I did hear that there are some predators in the Talic Region that the traders would speak a little about. Most of them wouldn't say much. The look of fear on their faces said more than any amount of words.

"And, of course, you have all the little things like the bugs and the poisonous bushes and berries and more. Oh, yeah, and the Shaloomd. We'll probably see some of those first."

"What are the Shaloomd?" Ellcia asks, struggling a bit with the word.

Rulf turns around and takes in the area as if he hasn't heard the question. Not far ahead are some boulders set just off the road. He moves off in that direction, and we all follow. When we reached the spot, we see that it must be a common area used by travelers. There's an area in the middle where countless fires have been lit, and off to the side, the grass is flattened out and mostly dead. I suspect it's from bedrolls or tents.

We settle down and pull out some food. It's late afternoon and a little early for the evening meal, but we missed having a break of any kind during mid-day.

We wait a while for Rulf to answer Ellcia's question, but he seems to have forgotten. Finally, I pipe up and say, "So, about Ellcia's question. The Shaloomd?"

Rulf nods. "Oh, yeah. The Shaloomd."

He pauses again for a long time. I find that kind of thing irritating. He seems to like to sit there and say nothing while we wait. I'm beginning to think he's forgotten again when he finally speaks up. "The Shaloomd are birds."

"Ahhhh!!!!" Marleet screams.

I jump to my feet and pull out my dagger. Everyone else is on their feet in a second, and we all face outward, ready to defend.

"What is it, Marleet?" Ellcia asks. "Are you hurt?"

"No! I'm not hurt! I'm frustrated! Rulf! You need to start answering questions. NOW! We need more information!"

I put my dagger back in its sheath. I'm tempted to chew Marleet out for scaring us, but I feel the same way. Rulf is too difficult to get information out of. Maybe he'll listen to Marleet. He seems to have a bit of a soft spot for her. She can be annoying at times, but she's also one of the nicest people on the planet.

"Oh. Sorry about that."

We all sit back down, and Rulf takes a mouthful of food. He chews it slowly while he collects his thoughts. When he finally speaks, he says, "The Shaloomd are birds. They're large and have a wingspan about the height of an average man. About Caric's height or a little less. They eat anything from mice to rabbits, but they can actually kill and eat a human."

I find myself searching the sky, and I see everyone else doing the same, aside from Rulf. "So," I say, "we're all in danger of one of these birds coming down to eat us?"

"Well," Rulf replies, "not exactly."

We wait for a bit, and then Hemot says, "This is one of those times when we're expecting more information."

"Oh, right." Rulf looks genuinely surprised. "I mean, some of you are in danger. I'm not. No Shaloomd can pick me up. They don't really attack. They grab you and try to take you up into the sky. If you struggle and fall out of their talons, you'll plummet to your death, and they'll take your lifeless body to their nests. If you don't get out of their talons, they'll just take you alive to their nests. Once there, they'll eat you. You can fight them off, but there are a lot of them up there."

"Is there anything we can do to avoid being grabbed by one?" Ellcia asks.

"They tend to only hunt creatures who are alone. If you see one in the sky, stay really close to one another. Don't go off by yourself for any reason."

"What about…" Marleet says, looking quite uncomfortable. "What about… when we… have to… you know… relieve ourselves?"

Rulf nods slowly. "That could be a problem."

Marleet throws her hands up in the air and shouts, "So, what do we do about that?"

"Just make sure the two of you go together," he says, pointing at Ellcia and Marleet. "But, you're in the most danger," he says, fixing his gaze on Marleet alone.

"Why me?" she asks in a small voice.

"Cause you're so much smaller and skinnier than anyone else," Rulf says. "You'll be the first one they target. They'll pick you up and carry you away with no trouble at all. We'll never see you again." He pauses for a moment and adds unhelpfully, "You'll be an easy Marleet-shaped snack for them."

Marleet's face fills with a look that's halfway between terror and... well... nope... that's just terror. Sheer terror. Hemot slides a little closer to her and glances up at the sky with an angry look in his eye, like he's mad at the birds already.

"How do you know all this?" I ask. "You've never been out of the city before."

Rulf shakes his head and then stands up. "I've been out of the city before, but we need to move."

We get up and return to the road. I see traders off in the distance moving toward us, but they're still far enough away that I can't even make out how many there are.

Once we're moving again, Rulf says, "I've been out of the city three times before now. Once when I was an infant. I was only two months old, and I barely remember it. I was only speaking a few words."

I shake my head, partly out of amazement and partly out of frustration. Something about a two-month-old Rulf speaking annoys me. The image in my mind is also a little disturbing. I wish he was a little more like the rest of us.

"The second time, I was over a year old, so I remember everything, but I didn't learn too much. My mom kept me close by. The third time was just before I turned two. My dad took me out camping. That's when I learned how to set snares."

"You do know that most people can't learn to set snares at two years of age, right?" I ask. But then I add, "But what about everything else? All the other stuff you know."

"I read a lot. And I listen to traders."

"You talk to traders?" Marleet asks. "But you don't talk very much at all."

"I listen."

"Good listener. Good listener," Mic says. "Hears everything. Hears everything."

"And how come the dogs didn't hurt you?" Ellcia asks. "They would have torn any of us to pieces."

"I have tough skin," Rulf growls and pulls ahead of us. From the way he walks, I know the conversation is finished.

We wander on, and it feels like we're making little to no progress. The landscape remains the same with small, rolling hills, covered in grass and the occasional forest in the distance. Ahead of us, I think I see what appears to be a rockier section of land.

"They're here. They're here," Mic says.

I turn around, expecting to see the assassins, but there's no sign of them. A shadow passes over me, and I look up to see a large, black and gray bird with nasty looking talons and a vicious beak. It's only about a stone's throw above us. I assume that's the Shaloomd, and it's just as terrifying as I could have imagined. I don't know how it crept up on us.

I feel Ellcia step up next to me on one side, and Hemot and Marleet pull up next to me on the other side. Mic makes his way over to Rulf, who pulls back near the rest of us. "They'll be on us for a while," Rulf says. "You all have to be careful. I'm not sure, but the bigger ones might be able to take any one of you."

"Wait," Ellcia says. "If this thing flies above us, isn't that like waving a big flag and screaming out, 'Hey assassins! We're over here!'"

"Yup," Rulf says.

"How long will it follow us?" I ask.

"I think they tend to remain more on the west side of the Talic Region. They don't like the mountains, from what I hear. But they aren't our biggest problem right now."

"What?" Marleet hollers. I didn't know her voice could reach that pitch, nor had I previously known what it would be like to have her holler like that while standing so close to my ear.

"I'm more concerned about what's behind us," Rulf says.

I look back and don't see anything at first, but then I notice the problem. I can't see a danger following us, but not far behind us, three Shaloomd circle a short distance above the ground. Someone else is back there, and I expect it's the last two assassins.

Rulf glances back and says, "They're getting closer. And quickly. We have to pick up our speed."

We take off at a decent run, once again, but this time we remain close together. I end up taking Ellcia's hand, and Hemot grabs my other one. We're nearly tripping over one another's feet, and Ellcia's sword keeps swinging over and hitting my leg, but we have to stay close.

"We'll try to hide in the city ahead, or we'll take our stand there," Rulf calls back.

I look at the Shaloomd marking out our pursuers. I think they're gaining on us. At this rate, they'll catch us soon.

We come over a larger hill, and I'm shocked to see the remains of a huge city ahead. It spans over a massive distance, but it's all just rubble. The road itself moves through the city, and the whole area lays in what appears to be a shallow valley in the region.

As we run down the slope of the hill toward the city boundary, I already see there are few, if any, places in the city to hide. It's all just rubble. I expect this is one of the cities that angered a Reber Troll.

Rulf leads us into the city, or what's left of it, and down a main street. It looks like this road is one of the areas in the city not covered in rocks, boulders, and smashed lumber. It's hard to believe one creature could do such a thing.

I glance above us, and the Shaloomd is closer, so I pull Ellcia and Hemot in tight next to me as we run. Marleet is already practically hanging off Hemot's other side, so I'm not too worried about her. Mic sticks close to Rulf. The big guy will take care of his friend. There's no doubt in my mind about that.

We do our best to keep ahead of the assassins. So far, there appears to be no place to stop for a rest and no place to hide. I have a sneaking suspicion the men behind us will be able to run for longer than we can, so we're likely going to have to face them soon.

The road ahead turns sharply to the left, but I can see nothing past the turn until we reach it. We round the corner only to find another turn to the right. When we reach the turn, we find the road dips down steeply, and we charge forward.

I feel like I haven't stopped running since the moment we approached the Captain to volunteer as a Vanguard. As much as I've learned about the lies I've been told, I long to be back in the castle, cleaning statues. Deep inside, I know I just want to rest. I don't think I could ever actually go back.

We're halfway down the hill when we see it. Against the backdrop of rocks and boulders, its light gray skin doesn't stand out at all, but the turning head and the big black eyes catch our attention. We all come to a halt at the same moment and lower our heads.

"Just move along the road slowly, and maybe the troll won't care about us," Rulf orders.

As we walk carefully, the road takes us within a few steps of the Reber Troll's outstretched leg. We step past it, and I'm surprised by the smell. There's an odor of mildew mixed with sweat that almost makes me gag, but I hold it in. The last thing I want is a Reber Troll after me.

We're just about past the troll when I take a quick look at it. I don't mean to, it just happens. I nearly scream as I see the eyes of that thing looking right at me, but I drop my gaze immediately. I wait for it to come after me, but breathe a silent sigh of relief after a moment when it doesn't move.

I hear the footsteps of the assassins coming from behind. They're moving quickly. I think we're nearly at the point where we can start to pick up speed again when I hear a roar. It's too far away to be the Reber Troll, but whatever it is, it certainly isn't friendly. I heard a roar of a lion once when a traveling circus had come to the castle to put on a show for us. It had scared me at the time, but I think I would prefer facing a lion than whatever made the sound that I just heard. This roar is loud, deep, and sounds as if it is a mix between a lion and a man screaming in rage.

I turn my head slowly to look behind me. I hope I'm far enough from the Reber Troll that I won't upset it. A moment later, two men come barreling around the corner. They're each covered in blood, and I don't think they care about us anymore. There's something terrible chasing them, and they only want one thing: escape.

"Move a bit faster, everyone," Rulf says quietly. "Try not to upset the troll, but what's chasing those men is not something we want to face either."

"What is it?" I whisper as we pick up speed. I glance back again to see the men have reached the bottom of the hill and will soon pass the troll.

"Talic Wolf," Rulf replies. "We're meeting just about every danger I think the Talic Region has to offer."

We pick up speed, but I dare not break into a run just yet. I fear the assassins, however. They may be more concerned with getting away from the Talic Wolf than they are with killing us, but I'm guessing they won't pass up an opportunity to finish the job as they run past.

I look back just as the first assassin reaches the Reber Troll. The man doesn't seem to have noticed the troll. I would think he'd at least notice the way we're acting and try to find out why we aren't running, but the look of panic on his face tells me he's not thinking straight.

When the man reaches the point of the troll's foot, a giant hand stretches out and grabs him, lifts him easily into the air, spins him around, and slams him face down onto the road. The second assassin grinds to a halt and tries to scramble away, but the troll grabs him too and raises him up to its mouth.

I turn my head, and we pick up our speed just a little more. We reach the corner just as I hear the troll stop chewing. Once we're out of sight of the creature, we take off at a run again.

Rulf pushes us on even faster than before. "We need to get out of here. The Talic Wolf likely won't care about us, but if it sees us, it'll come after us. You don't want one of those after you."

"Won't the troll kill it?" Ellcia asks. "It killed those men!"

I hadn't realized that Ellcia had been looking back. She sounds quite upset. I make a note in my head to talk to her later about it. I know her well enough to know she'll struggle with that. I think I'll struggle as well but talking to her will help me too.

"No," Rulf says. "The wolf will avoid the troll. The troll won't be able to catch the wolf—perhaps ever—but it'll follow the wolf everywhere and destroy everything the wolf does. Talic Wolves don't like that kind of thing. Let's just hope the wolf doesn't know about us yet."

11

The Talic Wolf

At the end of the next day, we find a small forest about a mile off the main road and make our way over to it. It's farther than we want to go from the path, but a forest should mean small animals for Rulf to catch and likely a water source.

I lean back against a fallen log with Ellcia and Marleet, and we chat about how our feet don't hurt quite as much as they did the first few days. It's nice to talk about unimportant stuff. We haven't had any danger or threats since the day before when we saw the end of the assassins.

Neither Ellcia nor I have talked about what we saw. It bothered me a lot, but the truth is, the thing that bothers me the most is that I'm happy the assassins are dead. I wonder what's wrong with me that I would feel this way.

Mic sits off by himself. He never really engages much with any of us. It's hard to even remember him, because of his armor, but when we try to talk to him when Rulf isn't around, he pulls away and sometimes covers his head. We've left him alone for the most part. Marleet keeps trying to reach out to him and once even gave him a long hug. He didn't seem to mind the hug this time—in fact, he seemed to like it—but he pulled back after and stayed away from her for the rest of the day.

His big bruise on his face is just about gone. I've never actually seen him without either a large bruise or covered in mud and dirt. He hasn't been rolling around in the mud, so hopefully he'll stay a little cleaner.

I had heard that Rulf was the one who gave him the bruises all the time, but it's starting to look like it was someone else all along.

As the light begins to fade, Rulf and Hemot come back into view. The evening before, Hemot had asked Rulf to teach him how to set snares, and Rulf had grunted his disapproval. Hemot had misinterpreted Rulf's reaction and just took it as a resounding yes. Rulf seemed annoyed at first, but by the time they came back, the big guy appeared to have a smile on his face. Hemot has that effect on people. He wears them down. He either wears them down to a happy point or an angry point. I'm glad it seems to be more "happy" with Rulf.

When Rulf and Hemot sit down, we all dig into a meal, which consists of a bit of cheese left over from somewhere. I've lost track of where we got all our food. Most of what we have left came from the other Vanguards, although we have some dried pork that we bought off a merchant traveling along the road. We also have a small amount of rabbit left from Rulf and Hemot's catch the night before.

"Are you really only fifteen?" Marleet asks, interrupting the silence.

Rulf grunts and says, "I am. I've always been big for my age."

I settle in for tonight's conversation. It's ended up being a bit of a daily routine for us. We sit down and pelt Rulf with questions. Sometimes he answers; sometimes he doesn't. Often, his answers create more questions. But whether he answers or not, it breaks up the monotony.

Hemot dives in next. "I had heard in the city that you were descended from giants. Is that true?"

Rulf is silent at first. He doesn't normally like answering questions, let alone questions about himself. He's often quite difficult when it comes to those topics. I think that's why we push so much in that area. It's like a challenge to get something from him.

After a few minutes, he finally says, "Yes. My great-great-grandfather fell in love with a giant."

It's now our turn to be silent. I had heard the rumors many times and even spread them a little myself, but I never actually believed it—well, until recently. But even then, there was a lot of doubt. Finally, I say, "Really?" I look over at Ellcia to see she's struggling with the same thing I am. I've never seen a giant before, but I've heard of them. I've even seen drawings of them. They don't seem like something your average man would fall in love with.

Hemot appears to be emboldened by his recent win at getting an answer out of Rulf, so he takes it a step further. He says, "I thought giants were really, really, really ugly."

Rulf roars in rage, but then stops as if he's trying to control himself. He looks around at each of us, but I gather we're all thinking the same thing. We're thinking that Hemot shouldn't have said that, but now that he did, we'd kind of like an explanation. The pictures I had seen of giants were hideous. They're roughly twice the height of an average man, have thick impenetrable skin, big square teeth in a massive mouth, and they drool a lot—a LOT.

Rulf relaxes his body a little and frowns. He's normally frowning, so what passes over his face is more like a deeper frown than just a frown. Finally, he says, "Well, he fell in love with her for her mind."

I find my lips do something funny. I'm not sure exactly what they're doing, but it feels like a cross between a frown and a smile. I look over at Ellcia and see her lips are doing what mine feel like they're doing. I'm not going to say the obvious. I normally like it when we push Rulf to answer questions, but I'd kind of like it to end there.

Unfortunately, Marleet speaks up. Her eyes are unfocused as she stares off into nothing, obviously trying to work through her confusion. In a quiet voice, she says, "I thought giants were extremely dumb."

Rulf leaps to his feet and moves for Marleet. Before I know what's going on, I'm standing between her and Rulf, and Ellcia is standing behind me with Marleet behind her. Hemot stands in front of me, and he has both fists up in the air, as if that would do anything to stop Rulf.

I'm not sure if Rulf is going to attack, but the look on his face says he wants blood. I guess the comment about giants being ugly is one thing, but to call his great-great-grandmother dumb is too much.

Before Rulf can decide what to do, Mic steps in between. With an urgent tone, he says, "Bad hit girl. Bad hit girl."

Rulf glances down at Mic and then returns to his seat on a fallen log. He grinds his teeth—loudly—and clenches his fists, but he stays where he is. The rest of us slowly return to our seats. Everything feels tense, and I fear Rulf will charge again at any moment.

We all sit still. I dare not move or say anything. Rulf hasn't responded that way to a question for a while, and even then, it wasn't toward Marleet. After a few awkward moments, Rulf clears his throat. I watch as his face moves from angry, to uncomfortable, to awkward. Then his face does something that at first terrifies me, then confuses me. The next thing I know, he's broken into laughter. The rest of us join in, and we all have a good laugh.

We finish up our meal and then practice a little sword fighting with sticks, then with our actual swords. I don't dare use my sword against any of them, however, as I'm afraid that it'll chop right through the other's swords, or if I miss their sword, I'll kill one of them.

When we're finished, just in the fading hours of the evening, Mic steps up to Rulf. He grabs him and pulls him into the forest. He's not done this kind of thing before, but I can see that Mic wants to talk to his friend. They go just far enough that I can't make out any words they say. From the way Rulf paces back and forth and Mic waves his arms, they're obviously arguing. I want to go see if they're okay. I'm not afraid for Mic. Rulf treats him well and seems willing to do anything for the guy, but Rulf can be unpredictable.

Their arguing gets more and more intense, and I can see Rulf grow agitated. He begins to stomp his feet and shake his fists. Something Mic says is making Rulf very angry. I don't know what I can do, but I'm just about to head over there to see what's going on when Rulf backhands Mic right across the face.

My heart goes cold as I see Mic knocked back so hard his feet actually leave the ground, and he crashes down into the underbrush.

I rush forward and reach him. He's unconscious, and Rulf shakes with rage. I want to yell at Rulf, but I'm too scared. I've never seen Rulf so angry before.

Ellcia and the others reach us, and before they can argue with Rulf, I ask them to help me get Mic back to camp. I don't want any of us trying to talk to Rulf when he's in this state.

As we try to lift Mic's unconscious body, Rulf steps forward and pushes each of us out of the way. He kneels next to Mic and gently picks the boy off the ground. Tears flow down Rulf's cheeks, but I can see he's still enraged. He takes Mic back to camp, sets him gently down on his blankets, covers him up, and then walks a short distance into the forest and drops to the ground. We hear Rulf sob loudly as he lays in the darkening woods.

The next day, I awake before the rest to find Rulf cooking his recent catch over the fire. I try to talk to him about what happened, but he's gone back to his typical grunts and growls. I'm not sure I'll ever understand him. Maybe it's the giant blood in him. How can anyone go from laughing with us to beating his friend to weeping alone on the floor of the forest?

When everyone else wakes up, including Mic, we eat a portion of what Rulf caught and then head out. Mic's face has swollen up, and it's obvious now that his swollen face of the past was always the result of Rulf. The guy scares me, but I'm angry at him as well.

Marleet tries to tend to Mic's face, but he pushes her away. He seems to want nothing to do with her today.

I don't know how to react, but I'm not the only one. Ellcia looks like she wants to chew Rulf out, but then she keeps pulling back. I think we're scared of Rulf now, but we need him. I'm just not sure what the right thing to do is.

We move on in silence for most of the day, bunching together as we walk to keep the Shaloomd from grabbing anyone. Two Shaloomds circle above us for most of the day, but they're far enough up there that I don't think they see us as a likely meal. I expect, however, that if one of us wanders away from the group for even a second, the birds will drop down quickly to see if they can take advantage of the situation.

Mic has taken up position next to Rulf again. At one point, he slips back a bit, and I ask him if he's okay. He just responds with, "It's okay. It's okay." Then he runs up again to join Rulf.

We move on through the day with little to nothing of interest happening. I keep my eye on Rulf and Mic the whole time, but they seem to get along fine.

A nice breeze blows from the west, and the sky is cloudy. It makes for good traveling weather. By late afternoon, we're on the lookout for another forest where we can camp for the night. We find a small stream running near the road, so I figure we don't need a forest, but Rulf tells us the trees will protect us from the Shaloomd. Otherwise, we'll have to sleep nearly on top of one another or risk waking up with one or two of us missing. Again, he reminds us that it wouldn't be him that the Shaloomd would eat.

I spot what looks like a forest in the distance, and we push forward. It looks like the road runs within half a mile of the treeline. I like the idea of not having to trek so far off the road to find a place to camp for the night. Every step we take away from the road is one step we have to travel back again.

By this point, my feet are a little sore from walking all day, but I no longer have blisters… or I no longer feel them. When we reach the area of the road close to the forest, we move off the road and make our way to the trees. We settle in for the night.

The next day, we set out early. Rulf has already caught, skinned, and cooked four rabbits, so we're able to eat right away and get going. It's nice to know we have a little extra food. When we reach the road, we head east again. The mountains still don't look any closer, but I know in my head that we've covered a lot of ground.

This day's travel seems no different from yesterday's at first, but around mid-morning, everything changes.

My heart fills with terror as we hear something that we haven't heard for three days. A loud roar erupts from the south. It's the same sound we heard when the assassins met their fate with the troll—the sound that Rulf said was a Talic Wolf.

"Run!" Rulf hollers. He grabs Mic and me and drags us off down the road. When I can get my feet under me again, I push Rulf's hand away and run alongside Ellcia, Marleet, and Hemot.

"Did we disturb it?" Hemot calls out.

"No!" Rulf says. "It's probably been hunting us since that ruined city."

"If it's hunting us, why did it roar?" I ask. "Didn't it just announce its presence?"

"No!" Rulf hollers again. "The roar announces the hunt has begun. A Talic Wolf always announces its hunt once it's fully underway. It does that so we can run. It likes a chase."

We race down the road as Rulf gives us a bit more info. None of what I hear sounds good.

"Few people have ever killed a Talic Wolf," Rulf says. "It doesn't fear swords or arrows or spears. The only thing it fears is fire. I read a story once of a man who ran a spear through the heart of a Talic Wolf. The wolf just laughed and killed the man while his friends watched."

"The wolf can laugh?" Marleet hollers out. "The wolf can laugh?! Does no one else think there's something wrong with that?"

I do think there's something wrong with that. Not that Rulf is wrong. As much as I'm angry at him for hitting Mic, he's been right about just about everything so far. I just don't think wolves should be capable of laughter.

"Is it fast?" I ask.

"Really fast," Rulf replies. "We can't outrun it."

"What?" I holler. "Then should we just give up?"

"No," Rulf growls. "The Talic Wolf likes the hunt. It will chase us for as long as it's enjoying itself. Only when it gets bored will it attack. If we ignore it, we'll likely be dead by noon. So, we have a chance of getting away as long as it's having fun. We have to make it to sundown. A Talic Wolf only hunts during the day. During the night, it eats and sleeps."

"It eats at night?" Hemot asks. "What happens if it catches us during the day?"

"It'll keep you until the sun sets," Rulf explains. "If we can manage to keep away from it until dark, then we can travel all night and get far away from it. If we can reach Leito City, we might lose it."

We run on through the rest of the morning and continue as the afternoon passes by. The sun is still far from setting, but it is getting low in the sky. Now and then we hear the wolf howl again. Sometimes the sound comes from behind us. Sometimes it comes from the north or the south. There are either multiple wolves, or the creature is toying with us. I'm not sure which option I prefer.

After hours of running, we're all exhausted, but I'm impressed with how well we're doing. Day after day of running really does a great job of building endurance. My legs no longer feel weak, and my back is no longer as sore. The pack actually doesn't feel all that heavy anymore.

The Wolf roars again, but this time, it sounds like it's right behind us. I holler out, "If it catches us and keeps us until dark, does that mean we'll have a chance to escape before the sun sets?"

Rulf growls. "No! There will be no chance to escape. A Talic Wolf is too smart. It'll guard its victim well. But the good news is that it's not after all of us. There's always only one in the group that it wants. It'll have picked its prey, and the rest of us might be safe."

"That doesn't sound like overly good news to me," Marleet says as she gasps for air. "I think that's just not-as-bad news."

Rulf only grunts in reply.

"If it catches me, I'll fight it off with everything I've got!" Hemot says.

"Best of luck with that!" Rulf says. "I hear the Talic Wolf's speech is terrifying. Few people can manage to keep their courage when it speaks."

"This wolf laughs, and it speaks?" Marleet hollers. "It's an abomination!"

"I have to agree with Marleet on that," I say. "I really don't think something like that should exist."

We've settled into a fast jog. I'm pretty sure that no speed is going to be fast enough to stay away from this thing, but we have to keep moving.

"Wait," Ellcia says, as we all run. "If it speaks, maybe we can reason with it."

"No!" Rulf yells. Sometimes, too many questions upset him. "Talic Wolves don't see humans as intelligent. Humans are only food to them. They love to have a conversation with us, but the wolf will not consider any compromise for even a moment. People say the Talic Wolf enjoys chatting with its meal before it eats it."

"Then some people have escaped!" Ellcia says. "Otherwise, we'd have no idea that it likes chatting with its food!"

I find myself smiling, despite the circumstances. I hadn't thought of that. Leave it to Ellcia to catch that kind of thing. By the look of Rulf's reaction to Ellcia's comment, it sounds like he hadn't thought of it either.

"I don't know, but none of that matters right now," Rulf says. "What's important is that we have to get away. Now!"

We run on into the late afternoon. If we can keep the pace until dark, we might have a chance.

12

The Flight

We push on through the night and into the next day.

For most of last night, we walked at a fast pace, trying our best not only to gain some distance, but to conserve our energy. While it was dark, we didn't hear a single roar. We thought we were getting away.

Once morning hit, we started to jog again, and we ran late into the morning. By mid-morning, my legs no longer really felt like they were a part of me. They felt like they were running without my permission.

About twenty minutes ago, I started to feel sorry for myself. This entire journey has been one deadly experience after another. While I don't think I could ever go back to work in the castle under the Regent, I once again dream of how simple life used to be. The only good news is that the Shaloomd have backed off. It seems they don't want to mess with the Talic Wolf any more than we do.

Around noon, we all come to a complete halt.

We wouldn't have stopped at all, except that twenty paces in front of us, the Talic Wolf has stepped out into the middle of the road.

It's large. It's bigger than any dog I've ever seen, and its shoulders are as wide as a horse. The paws look like a lion's and the snout is wide. As it snarls, its gleaming white teeth make an appearance.

Rulf has his sword out, and the rest of us follow his example. Mic grabs his crossbow and drives a bolt into the chest of the beast, but it barely seems to notice. It casually reaches down with its mouth, grabs the end of the bolt, pulls it out, and tosses it aside as if it's not concerned.

"Leave us alone, Wolf!" Rulf hollers.

The wolf laughs. The sound comes out slow, raspy, and filled with disdain. The creature paces back and forth, and I'm pretty sure it's smiling. The red eyes look both hungry and happy.

We stare at it for a few minutes. It doesn't do much other than pace and smile, and we don't dare move. I can't help but think that it wants us to run in the other direction, but there's no benefit to that for us. Our only hope is to maintain our distance until dark, then try to reach Leito. It's doubtful, however, that we can achieve either.

I remember that my sword is different from the others. I can't help but think that while the others might struggle to harm the beast, I might actually be able to kill it. Maybe it takes an enchanted item to kill an enchanted beast. So far, my sword has been capable of slicing through anything. I doubt that wolf can survive an attack from it.

I step forward and take my stand between the wolf and my friends. I think the smile on the wolf's face grows larger as I do this, which is quite unnerving, but I'm not willing to back down.

"What are you doing?" Ellcia asks.

"I think with my armor and my sword, I might be able to kill it," I whisper back, trying to be as quiet as possible.

The wolf laughs again. This time, its laugh seems worse than the first time. I'm beginning to see what Rulf was talking about. It enjoys its prey. It seems to like it when we speak or try anything, but it doesn't think much of us.

Without warning, the Talic Wolf charges. I tense up as the creature moves like lightning, and I take a big swing with my sword.

But it's too quick.

The last thing I remember is tumbling and crashing across the ground.

I awake and open my eyes. Before me is a wooden wall. I'm struggling to make sense of what I see, and all that's going on around me. I can hear someone breathing quietly behind me, but I don't know who it is.

As my memories flood back, I remember I had been on a search for the Prince, although the journey had not involved much searching, only running. We had been on the road, then… the Talic Wolf.

My eyes open wide, and my head clears. I feel a burning pain in my left arm—the one I'm lying on. I'm still in my armor and fully dressed. I thought at first that I might be somewhere safe, but I no longer think that's the case. No friend would leave my injured arm untreated, nor would they lay me on it while I slept.

The sound of someone breathing behind me…

I begin to think I know what's making that sound.

A voice breaks the silence. "Will you speak with me?"

The voice is creepy. It's low and airy, with a hissing sound coming out around the words. A deep rumble accompanies the voice along with a high-pitched whine. I've never hated a sound like the sound of that voice. Rulf was right. My courage is melting away.

I push myself up and sit straight. My head spins, and I have to take a moment to let it settle. I raise my right hand and feel the back of my head to find a large, bloody gash. I'm guessing that's where I hit when I lost consciousness.

I force myself to turn around, but it only makes the whole experience worse. The Talic Wolf sits not far from me. Its eyes are on me, but I don't think it's to make sure I don't get away. I think it's enjoying watching everything I do.

The room is large. It's all wood—wood floors, wood walls, wood ceiling. I think at one point it was the home of someone important. The tattered remains of curtains and tapestries and broken furniture speak of wealth long gone.

I glance behind the wolf at a large window. The glass is unbroken and faces west. Just a sliver of sun still peeks up above the horizon. It won't be long before it's dark.

The wolf turns its head just slightly as it stares at me with a curious look in its eyes. "Are you hungry?"

"Maybe a little," I say. I'm not really sure I want to have a conversation with the beast, but if it's showing me a little kindness, maybe it's not as dangerous as I thought.

"Can I get you a blanket so you can warm yourself?" It turns its head the other way just a little.

"No, thank you. It's quite warm."

"Yes, it is," the wolf says. "It often is this time of year. Are you hungry?"

I furrow my eyebrows in confusion. At first, I don't understand why it would ask the same question twice, but then I remember what Rulf said. The wolf likes to chat with its prey, but it doesn't consider us intelligent.

"Are you hungry?" I ask.

"Yes, thank you," the wolf says with a slow laugh. "I've never been asked that by a human before. Are you hungry?"

I frown at the creature, which only seems to make it happier. "My friends will come for me."

The wolf smiles. "I hope so. I won't likely need to feed for a few days after you, but it'll be fun to play with them while I digest. The one, however, looks like it is of giant spawn. I don't particularly like giant meat. It's too chewy and tastes a little like bark off a tree. It's not a pleasant meal."

"They'll kill you!" I say with a lot of emotion.

"Yes, I expect they will," it says, smiling again. "Would you like me to call a servant to draw you a bath?"

I reach for my dagger, hoping the wolf missed it, but when I glance down, I'm surprised my sword is in its sheath. I had just assumed the sword was lost to me as I had held it in my hand when the wolf attacked. I draw it out.

"Ahh, yes, your sword," the wolf says. "After I knocked you down, I retrieved it for you. Aren't I a nice host? Is there anything else I can get you to make your stay more comfortable?" It adds a laugh after its last question.

I grip the sword tightly in my hand and pull myself to my feet. The wolf doesn't back away or even move from its spot. It's not afraid of me at all, but it will be soon.

I step forward and plunge the sword deep into its chest. The mighty Talic Wolf's face twists, and it cries out in pain. I see its muscles ripple, and a look of terror mixed with agony flashes through its eyes. After a few seconds, however, it settles down and gives me a mocking smile. My hand is right near its mouth, and it simply licks my hand before asking, "Are you cold? Would you like me to fetch you a blanket?"

I yank the sword out of the beast's chest and swing it down on the wolf's neck. My sword slices clean through and out the other side. The head, however, does not roll. It's as if I had never attacked the wolf at all. There's no gash in its chest, nor is there even blood on the creature's neck.

"Would you like me to fetch you some slippers? I would hate for you to be uncomfortable. I will be eating you soon, and I would so love to make your final minutes of living as happy as I can."

It laughs and steps forward. My sword has done nothing to the wolf, and I find I'm too terrified to do anything but stand there. It licks my left arm where I've been injured. A deep, satisfied growl emits from its throat.

It whispers to me, "It's almost time," and returns to its spot a short distance away. It sits again and watches me closely, a large smile on its face.

"Are you going to eat me?" I ask. I know the answer to the question—it just told me a moment ago—but despair has filled my heart, and I don't know what else to say or ask. The wolf only answers with a smile. I hate the next question, but I'm scared, and I must know. "Will you make it quick?"

The wolf shakes its head and laughs. "No, Your Highness."

I clench my teeth. My first thought is that it's speaking to me like Hob had, but I think it's only mocking me. However, I ask anyway. "Why do you call me that?"

"Because, Your Highness, I've tasted your family's blood before."

"My family's blood?"

"Yes, Your Highness. I have tasted your family's blood. Every family's blood tastes different. Royal blood tastes sweeter than some, yet saltier than others."

"I'm not royalty." I'm not sure I really believe that anymore, but I'm feeling stubborn. There's just a sliver of sun showing above the horizon. I can't see any way of killing this thing, but I can at least resist with my words.

"Oh, young princeling," the wolf says, "you certainly are royalty. You are related to the royal line of Sevord. I don't know how close you are to the throne, but guessing from your armor and your sword, I would say you are close. I have faced a man many years ago who was also a princeling. He was about your age and wore that leather armor and carried that same sword. From the taste, I would say he was your father or grandfather. He escaped me, which I regretted for many years, but no longer. If I had eaten him, his cub would never have existed. His escape promised me my meal today. So, I am grateful to him. When you see him next, thank him for me."

At that, the wolf laughs quite hard.

A flash of movement catches my eye, and I cover my face as something smashes through the window. When I uncover my eyes, a lit torch lies on the floor by my feet. I grab it and swing it at the wolf, and the creature backs away, snapping at me and growling.

"I will not give you up, princeling!" the Wolf growls. "I know your blood, and I will hunt you till the end of your days!"

I hear footsteps on stairs, and Rulf and Ellcia burst through the doorway. They each carry a torch and wave them to scare the wolf away. The creature had no fear of my sword, but the fire terrifies it.

While it tries to back away, Rulf steps right up to it and drives his torch into the wolf's side. The wolf screams and retreats to the far side of the room.

Ellcia is by my side and pulling me toward the door. Once we're through, she tosses her torch down on the floor, right in the doorway. I suspect on the dry wood, it won't be long before the floor starts to burn.

We rush down the stairs, and with each step, I smell more smoke. By the time I get to the bottom and run through an open doorway, the building is nearly engulfed in flames. Hemot, Marleet, and Mic run back and forth between a bonfire and the house, carrying logs and sticks on fire.

From the second floor of the large building, I hear a scream of rage. The wolf sounds terrified, but has no way out.

"Move!" Rulf shouts.

We rush away from the building. I feel lightheaded as we run, and it leaves me stumbling. Ellcia tries to help, but it just makes it worse and makes her stumble as well.

All around me are smaller buildings—none of them as large as the one I had been in. We are in some sort of abandoned town. Most of the buildings are broken down, and all of them surround the structure I had been in. I glance back to see that the Talic Wolf's home is fully on fire. A panic washes over me as I see the wolf smash through a window on the second floor and land on the ground. It howls, and its fur is on fire.

"We only have a few minutes," Rulf says. "I had hoped the wolf would die in the fire, but it didn't. It's going to be really mad."

"More angry than it already was?" Hemot asks with a sarcastic tone.

"Before, it would only have killed Caric," Rulf says. "Now it'll want all of us dead."

"Can we make it to Leito in time?" I ask.

"Leito is to the south. We've been tracking you for far enough that we might as well head to Haner now. We're a long way from the main east to west road."

Rulf leads us off through a small forest heading northeast. I had no idea the wolf had taken me far enough that we were closer to Haner than Leito, but that's good as we have to get to Morgin City anyway to look for the Prince—Haner is closer to our final destination. As we run, it strikes me that since we're the only Vanguard left, we really should explore each of the cities if we really want to find the Prince.

I pull myself back to the moment. There's no point in thinking about that kind of thing when we have a Talic Wolf after us. I hear its screams of agony mixed with roars of rage behind us. At the moment, the roars grow quieter. It'll be good to have the wolf far behind us. I'm hopeful the injuries it's sustained will be enough of a deterrent to following us. However, I tend to think Rulf is right. The wolf will be angrier now and willing to follow us to the very ends of the earth.

We reach the edge of the forest and break out into the open plains. The grass over the rolling hills is quite hard to run through. It's soft, which is kind of nice on the feet after walking on stone roads, but the ground is uneven, and the thick grass gets tangled around my feet. I nearly trip every few minutes, and I'm not the only one. Marleet goes down after a short while, and we stop briefly to make sure she's okay. Next, I go down, and everyone pulls me to my feet.

I'm in pain from where my head hit the ground when the Talic Wolf knocked me out and from my arm where the wolf bit me, but aside from that, I know I'm the most rested of the bunch. They've been running all day to rescue me. I feel grateful that they came for me. I had told the wolf they would, but I really wasn't sure. I'm not going to tell them that, though. I'll tell them how much I appreciate them rescuing me, but I'll keep my doubts to myself.

We run and walk through much of the night. It's quite peaceful, actually. Rulf tells us that he read that the Shaloomd mainly hunt during the day, so we should be safe from them. Even so, we stick close together as we move across the grasslands.

When the moon nears the horizon, we hear the Talic Wolf. It roars, then roars again. It's after us.

"I thought Talic Wolves only hunted during the day," Ellcia says, as we break into a run.

"I don't know," Rulf says. "I'm guessing if it's angry enough, it'll make an exception for us."

A few minutes later, we hear the roars and howls of the wolf grow quiet, only to find that a few minutes after that, it grows louder again. This continues on for what feels like hours.

Finally, Hemot glances back and hollers, "I saw it!"

We all turn around with swords drawn, but in the darkness, we don't see anything. "Are you sure?" I ask.

"Yes, it was over there!" He points at one of the smaller hills in the area. "It was just to the left of the peak."

We still don't see anything, so we move on, but a moment later, Ellcia catches sight of it. It's definitely tracking us, but it's acting odd. Even I can tell something isn't right.

A few minutes later, it runs out in front of us, and we all come to a halt. It walks back and forth once or twice, sniffing the air, but then takes off to the south at a run. Before it leaves our sight, it trips and falls, tumbling head over heels, then gets to its feet and takes off running to the west.

Rulf comes up close and whispers, "I think the fire really hurt it. It might be blind, and its sense of smell might be nearly lost. We're still in trouble, but not as much. It might only catch us if we stop. Or if we make too much noise."

"How far to Haner?" I ask.

"I'm not sure. I think if we keep moving, we should be there by mid to late afternoon."

I feel like groaning, but there's nothing that can be done other than run. We set off again, heading northeast. For the rest of the night, we catch repeated glimpses of the wolf, but it doesn't come too close to our position.

We push on as the sky in the east begins to lighten and turn to blue. When the sun peeks up above the mountains to the east, we slow down. It's shining nearly in our eyes, and we struggle to make our way without twisting an ankle or tripping over a larger rock or boulder.

Once the sun is fully up above the mountain peaks, I decide to take charge. Rulf seems content to keep moving, but none of the rest of us can manage much longer. No one argues with me about stopping, aside from Rulf.

We settle and eat what little food we have and drink most of the water we have left. I save a gulp or two as I don't want to be thirsty with no way to quench it. As we finish our meal, we remain still for a few moments. At first, no one says anything about one of our other big problems, but finally Marleet says, "What are we going to do about food? If the wolf is chasing us, we can't stay anywhere for the night and catch rabbits. Our cheese is now gone, and we haven't had bread for days."

Rulf remains silent. I think he's still angry about having to stop. Now and then, he glares at me.

I end up answering her. "We might be able to buy some food at Haner. Hopefully they'll let us into the city."

"Why wouldn't they?" she asks.

"I don't know. People can't travel in and out of the capital without permission."

"But we have the papers from the Captain!" She looks terrified.

"Yes, but I think those papers give us permission to get into Morgin City. They might not get us into Haner." I glance at Rulf, and the look on his face tells me that he hadn't considered that possibility.

"Can we kill the wolf?" Marleet asks, her voice just above a whisper.

Rulf stands to his feet quickly and growls. He looks at her and says, "Fire. The only thing that will kill it is fire. But we have no wood."

We look around and see he's right. There's a forest in the distance back towards the west, but there's no way we're going to retrace our steps back to that point. I do find it tempting, however. I think if we can kill the wolf, we can settle in at the forest for the day and catch some food. There's likely water there too.

"We have to move!" Rulf says.

As if on cue, the wolf howls in the distance. It sounds like the roar is coming from in front of us, but it doesn't matter. The wolf has been all over the place. It won't be long until it's behind us again.

We move off again as the sun warms up the day, and I begin to sweat. Living in the castle, I bathed often, but I haven't had the chance even once since we left. The smell has been getting pretty bad. No one's said anything, though. I think we all accept the fact that we stink.

We run over yet another hill, and I hear the wolf howling somewhere to the south. One of these times it'll get really close, but I don't know if that means it'll find us or if it will just run on somewhere else.

At the top of yet another hill, I catch sight of the city. It's ahead of us and to the left. It's large, although I'm not sure it's as large as Sevord City. I think the capitol is the biggest city in the nation. Hemot hollers for joy when he sees it, but Rulf turns us a little to the right.

"Why aren't we heading straight for the city?" I ask, doing my best to keep my voice steady and not gasp for air.

Rulf simply says, "The road!" and keeps running.

I stare ahead and make out a cart moving through the hills and assume the road is near. While the road is not as soft as the grassy hills, we'll certainly make better time moving on it.

We reach the road about a hundred paces behind the cart. It's moving at a steady speed toward the city as it's pulled by horses, and we follow behind. Just as we reach it, the Talic Wolf comes over a hill and slams into the side of one of the horses.

The horse screams as the beast attacks. The wolf doesn't appear to want to eat the horse, just kill it. A moment later, it attacks the second horse as the four riders on the cart scramble off and run back toward us.

Rulf turns to us quickly and says, "Don't tell them the wolf is chasing us!"

I'm about to ask why, but something about the look in his eye tells me this is non-negotiable. We all nod and slow down. At the moment, the wolf is ahead of us, and we don't want to run into it.

When the two men and two women reach us, we see they're all armed. None of them look like soldiers, though.

"Run!" they say. "It's a Talic Wolf!"

The wolf is still not able to track us, but it's obviously able to pick up a certain amount of sound or scent. The horses were enough to draw it in.

"It's acting strange," I say to the people. "Maybe we can get by it and to the city."

They stop and turn around, watching it closely. The wolf runs along the road in our direction, but nothing about it suggests that it's coming for us.

We scramble off the road and wait for it to pass behind us before we run on. A few moments later, we pass the cart. One of the men jumps up into the cart and grabs a bag. I hear a jingle of coins and suspect it's their money from whatever they were selling.

We run on as the wolf roars. I look back to see that it's coming in our direction. It slams into the cart, then stumbles its way over the horses. It's acting more focused now.

I see it move back and forth across the road, but this time it's tapping the ground with its paw. It moves along, tapping everywhere until it reaches the edge of the road. It then moves back the other direction. It's figuring out that it's on a road—not the grass. It might just guess that we're a short distance away and charge.

Sure enough, a moment later, it starts to move in our direction. It taps the ground now and then to confirm that it's still on the road, and it occasionally sniffs the air. It's tracking us. We might not have much time left.

"Caric!" Ellcia hollers.

I turn back toward the others. I've fallen behind. Ellcia has slowed down a bit for me, and I run to catch up. The four traders are far ahead. I expect they're more rested than any of us.

I glance over my shoulder as I catch up to Ellcia and see the wolf is significantly closer. It's still struggling to find its way, but it won't be long until it's upon us.

The city's not far ahead, and as we come closer, I'm impressed at the height of the walls. I suspect they're higher than the walls around Sevord City. Plenty of guards line the top, and even at a distance, I see spears and bows. The gate itself remains shut.

When we're within a stone's throw of the gate, a small door to the right of the massive main gate opens and six men run out. They have torches in their hands, and they take up position outside the wall. A seventh man then comes out and waves us toward him. The traders run in, and we follow without question. A moment later, we reach the door. I look back in time to see the six men with torches attack the Talic Wolf. I recognize the roar of anger and rage and pain that comes from the wolf. I feel sorry for it in a way, although I'm glad to be out of its reach.

13

The Day in Haner

We stand in the guardhouse, not daring to move. We don't want to upset the guards by slipping out before they check us out. I've heard of people who slip through the gates of Sevord without permission who are hunted day and night until found.

The sound of the wolf outside the gates can just barely be heard through the thick door—but I definitely can hear it. I think the memory of its roars and screams will cost me a lot of sleep in the days to come. I feel pity for the creature, but then I remember that it was just last evening that it tried to eat me.

One of the guards walks by us, and he gives us a funny look. I'm not sure when they're going to question us, but they seem to be in no rush. The two couples who entered ahead of us are nowhere to be seen. Whatever happened to them, happened fast.

We stand there for what seems like an hour before an older man in uniform comes and stands before us. He stares at each of us in turn. Rulf isn't pulling out the papers. I assume he knows what he's doing. I expect it's more a matter of not giving the guard anything he doesn't ask for.

"What?" the guard asks in a tone more like an order than a question.

He steps in front of me and leans in close. "You look like you're in charge."

I almost laugh but catch myself. I'm still at a loss for how to respond.

"What do you want?" he asks. "You're in the way. Do you plan to set up a tent? Maybe cook a meal?" He grinds his teeth for a moment before hollering, "Get out of my guard house!"

I turn and look for the door. It's not far away, and I give Ellcia a little push. She and the others rush in that direction. A moment later, we're out in the streets.

Once the door closes, Hemot speaks up. "I guess they don't check papers in this city."

Marleet seems to find that hilarious and giggles as we walk down the street.

I'm on the lookout for a market. We have plenty of money—at least I think it's plenty. I know the price of most things back in Sevord, but I don't know any of the prices in Haner. It might be a lot more expensive here.

We wander deeper into the city. Few people wear swords strapped to their belts. I'm grateful for ours as people appear to give us plenty of space. I had heard once that there were many thieves in the other cities, and I don't want to get robbed.

When we reach the market, I'm happy to find that everything is quite affordable. The money we found on the dead Vanguards is more than enough to pay for our food—not only for the day, but I suspect for many weeks.

We buy some food, although Rulf insists that everything we buy is what he calls "traveling food". We purchase salted meats, cheese, dried fruits, some kind of tough stale bread that's supposed to last, and anything we can find that won't go bad quickly. When we're finished,

154

we're stocked up for several days—even if we don't find any rabbits or squirrels.

None of us touch the food, although we're all hungry. Instead, Rulf heads out of the market area and down one of the side streets. We seem to be in an area filled with shops selling everything from clothing to baskets. After a short walk, he motions toward a large building. I see above the door a sign with one simple word on it: Inn.

I shake my head at how Rulf is able to navigate his way through just about every situation, except the one in the guardhouse. His reading and listening have prepared him well. Now and then I wonder how someone descended from a giant could be so smart. The fact that giants aren't the brightest of the enchanted creatures is a well-known fact, but then again, it *is* an enchantment. The little I know of those things, they're entirely unpredictable.

Rulf climbs the steps and pushes the solid door open, letting a waft of air rush out. The smell is a mix of fresh bread, roasted meat, and stew. All that smells good, but the aroma is spoiled by the intense smell of sweat. The sounds of laughter and arguing pour out into the street.

I step inside, and it takes me a minute for my eyes to adjust. There's very little light inside and the few windows are covered in either thick curtains or a layer of filth. Around fifty people have crammed themselves into this small space, but the scary part is that the laughter and arguing from a moment before has come to a grinding halt.

The eyes of every man and woman in the room have settled on us. I see them examine every detail, from our outfits and armor to our weapons and apparent strength. They seem to be evaluating whether to do anything about us.

After a full minute or so, a man hollers out, "We have visiting dignitaries!"

Everyone laughs, and we all look down. Sure enough, our outfits and armor are of a much finer quality than anything anyone else in the room wears.

We have a problem. If we were each twenty years older, we'd look like six dangerous soldiers. Since I'm the oldest among us and not even eighteen yet, we must look like we're pretending to be something we're not.

I briefly consider the fact that my sword can cut through anything and how that would scare off a lot of threats, but I then recognize that if these men knew what my sword can do, it would not be long before my sword would no longer be in my possession. I might also no longer be alive.

Rulf moves toward a large man behind a counter. I expect he's the innkeeper, or at least someone important. We follow and when we reach the counter, we lean up against it. Rulf growls, "Two rooms for the night. Meals in our rooms. What will that cost?"

The man laughs and says, "Well, young lad, that sounds like quite an order. Considering I'll have to pay the maid to clean your room…" that comment elicits a laugh from everyone, "and we'll also have to open up the kitchen and prepare a nice feast for all of you…" that also elicits a laugh, "I would think it'll cost just about everything you have, including your swords, knives, and armor." He stops and smiles before adding, "Yes, I think that would cover it."

A creak in the floorboards behind me causes me to turn around. Standing between us and the door is a large brute of a man. I don't really want to get into a fight, but if it's just one guy, I think we can handle him.

Rulf turns around and steps right up to the man. He grunts and then asks in a threatening voice, "What do you want?"

The man smiles and says, "I want to make sure I get a little piece of what Jebber over here is asking for. I fancy that sword that you're wearing, along with the sword the guy behind you is wearing." The man glances over at Mic.

One thing's for sure, I won't let him have Mic's sword. Mic has the King's sword. That should not fall into the hands of just any man. I briefly think back to what the wolf said to me and wonder if that sword actually belongs to me but push the thought out. I don't like thinking about that kind of thing.

I'm hoping we can find a peaceful way out of the situation, but that hope disappears as Rulf spits in the man's face. I hear Ellcia's frustrated groan beside me. This isn't going to go well.

The man wipes his face with his hand and then stares in disbelief at his palm. He looks back at the men behind him. No one laughs now.

I'm a pretty average height—if not a little taller than most—but Rulf makes me look small. The man before us, however, towers over even Rulf. His shoulders are wide, and his belly is huge. His hands look like they could wrap around my entire neck. His face is, unfortunately, contorted in rage.

He pulls back his arm and swings his fist, landing it square in Rulf's gut. Without meaning to, I holler out in shock. Rulf, however, barely moves—he barely even shakes.

The look on the man's face is one of shock, which likely bears a striking resemblance to the look I expect is on my face. I glance at the others, and all but Mic appear confused. Mic simply has a smile on his bruised and swollen face. I hear him mumble, "Don't hit Rulf. Don't hit Rulf," followed by a little chuckle.

"Oh," the man says, "you think just because you're wearing armor, I can't hurt you?"

Rulf smiles at the man. I haven't seen Rulf smile often, but when I have seen it, the look disturbs me. I actually prefer his frown. It feels far more natural.

Without taking his eyes off the man, Rulf undoes his leather armor and pulls up his shirt to reveal a bare stomach. The man smiles, glances back at his friends, lets out a little laugh, and says, "Ahh, you're up for more, are ya?"

He then reels back and slams Rulf in the belly. Once again, Rulf doesn't budge. I just can't believe Rulf can take that kind of abuse! At the very least, the power of that hit should knock Rulf back, but he remains perfectly still.

He drops his shirt back in place and does up his armor as the man watches in shock. He then growls loud enough for everyone to hear, "We don't want to be bothered. We want to be left alone." Turning to the innkeeper, he says, "We also want two rooms and our meal in our rooms for a reasonable price, or I might make an issue of this guy hitting me twice."

I hear a whisper move around the room and catch the words, "… giant blood…" The large man backs away, and the innkeeper asks for eight coppers for the rooms and another six for our meals. Rulf nods his head, tosses some money on the counter, and holds out his hand. A moment later, we have two keys and are on our way up a set of stairs at the back of the common room.

Our rooms are on the second floor of the inn. There's a third floor, and Hemot wants to go up there to see it, but halfway up the stairs we turn around. The stairs themselves are in such terrible condition that I fear we'll fall through the steps.

When we get back, we all settle down in Ellcia and Marleet's room, which is the larger of the two, and wait for our meals. It takes far longer than I would have thought, but I suspect they're not quick with anything in this inn.

When the meal comes, Rulf threatens the two women who bring the food. He tells them that nothing works on him, and if there's anything in the food that disagrees with him, he'll tear the inn down. They assure him the food is perfectly fine before running back down the stairs.

While I don't like the way he treats them, I had been worried that they would do something to our food to get back at us. This place seems far from safe.

When we finish our meal, we sit around and chat until the light fades. It's hard for me to believe that we could have so much to talk about after spending every moment together for nearly two weeks. Once the night settles in on the streets outside, we hear a few fights break out and decide to all sleep in the same room. We pull the mattresses from our room over, and Mic, Rulf, Hemot, and I sleep on the floor, while the girls sleep in the two small beds.

The next morning, we awake to horses charging through the streets. People are screaming, and I instantly know what the problem is. In the midst of the screams, I can hear the roar of the Talic Wolf. Somehow, it made it into the city.

"Time to move!" Rulf growls, and we scramble to our feet.

"How did it get past the walls?" Hemot asks.

I'm wondering the same thing. It's hard to believe it could get through all those men, let alone the wall itself. If the men are dead, and the wolf has killed people inside the city, I would feel so guilty about bringing it here. Another thought hits me as I'm packing up. Not only would I feel guilty, but the people of the city would consider us guilty. I see now why Rulf wants to get going.

We strap on our packs, but before we go, Rulf tosses some rolls of bread to each of us. We eat them quickly and drink our fill of water. It's time to run. Again.

We head down the stairs and past the sleeping innkeeper. Apparently, it takes more than screaming in the streets to wake the man. When we get outside, I suggest we head north. If we leave by the northern gate, we'll be on our way to Morgin City.

"No!" Rulf growls. "We head east."

He takes off down the road before I can argue with him. I've come to respect the big guy's decisions, but he sure does irritate me. I hope at some point he learns to actually get along with people.

We move through the streets, dodging people. Many run the same way as us, but others run opposite or across our path. It's clear no one knows which way to go.

As we run, we catch little bits of people's hurried conversations. Some people say that they heard the wolf has already killed over a hundred. Others say it's injured. One man says that he saw it, and it's barely walking.

We rush through the city, making our way east. After a while, I notice fewer and fewer people are moving in the same direction as us, then next to none. Finally, we find we're fighting against a crowd heading in the opposite direction. People holler at us that we're going the wrong way.

We step off to the side of the street and wait. There are too many to push against. I'm scared we'll run into the wolf, but I also know that the thing can't really see us, so even if we come across it, we might be safe.

The crowd thins, and we start to move toward the gate again. I see the wall over the top of the houses, and we're in the shadow of it as the sun hasn't risen enough yet to warm this part of the city.

We come around a corner to find dozens of soldiers with torches fighting the wolf. Its back two legs are no longer able to support its weight, and the front two legs drag its body along. The soldiers beat it with clubs and burn it with torches, but no one uses their spears. I remember how useless my own sword was against it.

The wolf screams almost continually, but also growls out the same words over and over. "Give me the princeling! Give me the princeling!"

The words are hard to understand, and I doubt anyone else quite catches what's said, but I sure do. I know he's after me.

We skirt around the soldiers and reach the wall, just south of the gate. Following along to the north, we eventually reach a group of soldiers. They look worried, but curious.

Before Rulf can growl at them, I speak up. Soldiers in Sevord tend to enjoy only two things: harassing people and listening to gossip. I'd rather avoid the one, so I dive into the other. "Quite the fight going on over there!"

"Did you see it?" a shorter, balding man asks. "Is it really a Talic Wolf?"

"Sure is." I tell him what we saw and shake my head. "They have it down, but that kind of thing is hard to kill."

"Never faced one myself," the man says.

"We have," I say, not mentioning that it was this specific one. "Barely got away with our lives. Not something I want to face again."

The man nods and looks at me with a newfound respect. "I would expect not!"

"Hey," I say casually. "We need to get through the gate. What time does it open?"

"Oh, not for another hour or so, but we can let you out through the guardhouse."

He waves for us to follow, and we move through a solid door, on through the guardhouse, and out another solid door. We thank the man, and I hear the door latch closed behind us. Ahead of us lies the mountains, green with snow-capped tops.

We just have to get around to the north and then on to Morgin City.

14

The Safe Walk

he road leading out of Haner heads to the east, directly toward the mountains. It's a decent size and well cared for, as I suspect they have much travel moving back and forth from the mines to the city, but at the moment, it lies empty. I vaguely remember learning about the mines in school. The mountains are full of copper. Some suspected the copper was the cause of the mountains being green, but no one really studied it. The copper was all that was important. I find myself wondering what life would be like if more people asked questions, but ironically decide to let it go.

I remember reading about how the miners would extract the copper from the earth, then bring it in long caravans to the cities. It would then be shipped west to be processed near the cliffs by the sea. If that was, in fact, how it was done, it's no wonder no one's on the road. There would either be dozens of carts when a shipment is moved or nothing at all until the next caravan sets out.

If I remember right, few others travel back and forth from the mountains to the cities.

We move east for a short distance as we can see a path heading north not far away. I hope we can take that and make our way around the city. Maybe we can connect with the main road heading north in a short while. If so, we might reach Morgin City in a few days and then begin our search for the Prince.

I feel a stab of fear in my heart at the thought of searching for the Prince… because more and more, I think I'm him. I don't want to think about it. I just want to be Caric. But then again, I kind of want to be the Prince. I imagine myself ordering the Regent's arrest. I wonder what it would be like to sit on the throne with Ellcia beside me.

I feel my face turn red, and for a moment, I think I might have said something about that out loud. I've never really talked to her about that kind of thing before, but I always assumed we would one day marry. A wave of panic washes over me as I wonder if she's considered that. What if she just thought I was her friend? Or worse! We don't really even know who we are. What if she turns out to be my sister?

"Are you okay?" Ellcia asks. "You look as green as the mountains."

I rush to the side of the road and empty my stomach and find Ellcia and Marleet come over and crouch by my side. I really don't want either of them to watch me do this.

"What's wrong, Caric?" Marleet asks as I pull myself to my feet.

I can't tell her why I'm throwing up. I'm not sure I'll ever be able to tell anyone why I'm feeling ill. I just shake my head instead, and they help me walk on. I already feel better, but I can't say that. I think I might have to pretend that I feel really sick for a little while just to help it all make sense for them, but I'm not sure how long I'll have to pretend.

I suddenly come to grips with the fact that I am a supremely odd person.

As we walk, Marleet rubs my back and says soothing things to me like, "You'll feel better soon," and "Don't worry; I've smelled worse."

I just want this day to be over.

We reach the small path heading north, and Rulf walks right past it without so much as a glance. Mic follows and doesn't stop.

Hemot is next to reach the path, as I'm still receiving emotional support from Ellcia and Marleet. He comes to a halt and calls out, "Hey Rulf, Mic! You missed our road!" When they turn back, he points and says, "Isn't this what we want? It'll be a long walk trying to get to Morgin City through the mountains."

Rulf grunts. "No! We're not going to Morgin City. We're going east."

I hang my head in frustration. I think this is going to be another one of those moments. Both girls take my action as a sign that I'm about to be sick again, and they lead me to the side of the road. I start to argue with them that I'm fine, but then I feel like I should oblige, so I empty what's left in my stomach.

I can't believe I just threw up simply because they expected me to do that! There's something seriously wrong with me!

Ellcia leaves me there with Marleet for a moment. While I don't particularly want to have Marleet by my side saying things like, "Don't worry, that happens to all of us when we vomit," at least I don't have Ellcia with me while I clean myself up. Besides, if anyone can argue with Rulf about the road to take, it's her.

"No, Rulf," she says. "We have to head north. Morgin City is where we're heading. Where are you planning on going?"

"The mountains," he growls.

"Why? We're after the Prince, right? That's what we're doing out here. Our job is to search Morgin City for him!" I hear the frustration in her voice.

Rulf walks a little toward Ellcia. He's a scary guy when he wants to be, but he always seems to listen to Ellcia.

"Girl," he says, addressing Ellcia. I suddenly wonder to myself if he's ever actually used her name. I think he mentioned my name once, but I think that might be it. Aside from Mic and me, I wonder if he knows the names of the rest of us.

Rulf continues in his gruff voice, "The Regent is our enemy. We aren't safe going where he wants us to go."

He lets that hang in the air for a moment. I know Ellcia doesn't like what he just said, but she knows Rulf's right.

Rulf continues, "We also know that the Regent doesn't want us to find the Prince—or at least to find him and bring him to the throne. Since the Regent doesn't want the Prince found, and he sent us to Morgin City, it's reasonable to assume the Prince is not in Morgin City."

I vaguely remember what the Captain said in his meeting with the Regent. Something about how none of them believe the Prince is in the cities.

Rulf takes a step closer to Ellcia, but not in a threatening way. It looks like he's actually trying to convince her, rather than just trying to bully the group into doing what he wants. "We can't continue among the common people. The Regent will hunt us down. At some point, someone will turn us over to him. We can live out in the wild for a time, but eventually we'll go a little crazy and eat each other." I find that statement somewhat concerning, but push it aside as Rulf continues. "The Regent has also very likely sent riders to all the cities to have us killed if we didn't die by the hands of the assassins. Therefore, we need to find a place to live that's outside of the regular cities and towns and villages. The mountains are the best place."

Rulf looks down for a moment as if he's considering whether to say something. When he speaks, he lowers his voice, despite how far we are from the walls of the city or any other people. "We're trying to stay alive, but more importantly, we need to make sure the Prince is safe. The Prince is not in the cities."

"Then where is the Prince?" Ellcia asks. I can tell she already agrees with him about heading east, but like the rest of us, we don't want to go that way.

"The Prince is," Rulf begins, but hesitates. When he speaks again, it is with a very solemn voice. "The Prince is either in the mountains or heading there."

At that last statement, his eyes make the briefest flick toward me. My heart jolts in my chest, but then feels like it turns to ice as I see that Ellcia also caught Rulf's glance at me.

As I wipe my chin, her eyes fix on me, and her mouth hangs open. A new understanding fills her face.

Hemot, missing all the subtle interactions, asks, "What makes you think the Prince might be in the mountains? I don't remember any rumors about him being that far out. I thought there was nothing but miners and giants in that area."

Rulf frowns at Hemot and then the big guy lets out a little growl. I'm not sure I know what's upset him, but he doesn't look like he wants to talk anymore.

Mic steps forward and pokes Hemot in the chest. "Go east. Go east."

He's right. I don't like it all, but Rulf's right. We can't go to Morgin City. The mining villages and the mountains are likely the best place for us.

I pick myself up, and we set off. We're still far from the mountains, but I'm hoping we can reach them soon. The landscape seems to be similar to much of the Talic Region, with rolling grass-covered hills and the occasional forest, but in the distance, there's a line of darkness before the foot of the mountains. I suspect it's a forest, and we'll be there soon enough. It would be nice to walk among the trees again. There's so much more life, and I like the shade. The sun grows hot in the open.

We trudge on throughout the morning and into the afternoon. The mountains don't seem to get any closer no matter how far we walk, but at least we're moving in the right direction. I'm surprised at how quickly we have all given up on heading to Morgin City, but then I think I also feel relieved. We might finally find some peace and be safe for a bit.

My mind drifts to what it will be like living in the mining villages. I've lived my entire life in a castle. I've seen drawings of the villages, and from what I've seen, it looks entirely like a big mud pit. I have a sneaking suspicion that life won't be all that comfortable.

I wonder if I will have to work in the mines. If I'm the Prince, does that mean I won't have to work? I can't imagine the Prince will just get to sit around and have everyone give him money. I realize I've never asked how a Prince actually becomes rich.

I also wonder if I'll have to lead the armies to war against the Regent. I'm not too keen on that. I had heard that the bulk of the King's army is out here somewhere. Maybe there will be generals who can lead for me, and I can ride at the back with Ellcia.

I roll the name around in my head—Prince Roran. Or… I guess King Roran would be better as it won't be long before I'll be crowned.

I stop that line of thinking. I feel silly. I may not be the Prince. In fact, I would prefer not to be the Prince. I want to just be me.

Now and then, Ellcia looks at me with a cross between wonder and confusion. I'm not sure I like either expression coming from her. Both make me feel uncomfortable.

By late afternoon, the mountains don't appear any nearer, and the forest in the distance, while closer, is still far out of reach. I can't help but think that we'll reach it late the next day or the day after.

I can just make out a smaller forest, one of the ones that dot the landscape of the Talic Region, a long way ahead.

When we reach the section of the road near the grove of trees, the sun is nearly set. The forest is about a five-minute walk from the road, so we make our way across the grassy land. When we get there, I see an odd-shaped structure among the trees. It's brown and looks like it's made of plaster. I'm about to ask what it is when Rulf growls extra loud.

I shake my head at him. At some point, he should learn to communicate less in growl and more in human speech.

Once we've all stopped, he points at the strange structure and says, "It's a hive."

Hemot perks up at the comment. "Then there's honey!"

"No!" Rulf says with far more rage than is necessary. "I'm not sure if they produce honey, but even if they do, you don't want to get it from them."

"Why not?" Hemot asks, taking a step forward.

"Those are Helio Bees," Rulf growls. "If you stay away, they don't bother you. But if you get close, they swarm you and attack in the thousands. No one survives."

He waves us to the east, and we walk along the edge of the forest for a while, doing our best to look for more hives. Rulf tells us that if there are no more hives, and if we stay on the other side of the forest, we should be okay.

When we're far enough away that I can no longer see the hives, Hemot grunts in anger. I turn to him, and I'm surprised by his expression. He never really gets that angry, but something is bothering him.

"What's wrong, Hemot?" I'm reminded of the fact that we haven't spent an awful lot of time together lately. Sure, we've been traveling side by side, but the two of us were always together in the castle. Now that we're out here, I'm spending all my time walking with Ellcia, and I miss Hemot.

Hemot grunts again and hollers, "Why is everything out here trying to kill us?"

Rulf stops and turns around, looking confused. He shakes his head. "Not everything. That caterpillar over there isn't trying to kill you." He points to a small gray little caterpillar on a large green leaf about an arm's length from Hemot. After Rulf's arm drops back to his side, he starts to let out a deep, slow laugh that goes on for an awkwardly long period of time. He seems to think he's said something funny.

When he finally stops laughing, I shake my head and prepare to move on, when Mic speaks up in a panic. He points at the caterpillar and says, "Don't touch. Don't touch."

Rulf steps a little closer to the leaf and then backs away quickly. "Wait, no. That caterpillar is poisonous. If you touch it, it secretes a poison that paralyzes you, and then somehow it calls its buddies. They come and eat you."

I roll my eyes and say with a lot of doubt in my voice, "Really?"

Rulf nods. "Not a fun way to go, from what I've read. It takes the caterpillars a good day and a half to finish you off, but they do. If anyone comes to your rescue, the caterpillars just end up having two meals instead of one."

"Should we find a different forest to stay in for the night?" Marleet asks. "Or even just sleep on the road rather than try the killer bee and killer caterpillar forest?"

Rulf looks unconvinced, but the rest of us just turn and walk back toward the road without waiting for his agreement. In a little while, we're back on the stone paved road heading east. The sun will set in a few hours, and I expect we'll be sleeping in the open tonight, but that's better than being eaten by caterpillars.

The next morning, I awake covered in webs.

I swing my arms up to bat off any caterpillars, and I'm relieved that I'm not paralyzed. I look around and see dozens of spiders quickly crawl away. A very unmanly sound emits from my throat as I scramble away from them. The others, aside from Rulf, aren't awake yet, and I'm grateful that they didn't hear the sound I made.

Ellcia, Hemot, Marleet, and Mic are also covered in webs, and I'm about to go try to brush them off Ellcia, when I realize that it won't go well if she wakes up to me doing that to her. I'm not sure how that conversation will go, so I'd rather avoid it. Rulf is nowhere to be seen, so I just holler out, "Time to get up, everyone!"

They all offer a similar reaction as they pull themselves out of their webs. The spiders don't appear to bite; they just seem to have felt we were worthy of making nests on. I check myself as best as I can to make sure I didn't miss any before I look around for Rulf.

In the distance, I see him moving toward us with something in his arms. I expect he caught us some food; he usually does. When he arrives, Mic already has the beginnings of a fire going, and Rulf sets about to clean his catch. Today, he found a slightly larger breed of rabbits than what we had in the grasslands, and I'm looking forward to a hot meal.

It's mid-morning by the time we move out. Normally, we try to get on the road a little earlier in the day, but I think we're all feeling exhausted from so many days of running for our lives. I'm hoping that we can have some time without a Talic Wolf or assassins or some other such life-threatening danger on our tail. Instead of running, I'd kind of like to just go for a walk.

It's a little cooler today, which is nice, but the reason worries me a bit. The sky has clouded over, and dark storm clouds move in our direction. The breeze feels good on my skin, and despite the oncoming storm, the refreshing weather is a nice break from what we've faced so far.

I find myself trailing behind the rest of the group with Ellcia. The Shaloomd haven't bothered us in a while, so we have a bit more freedom to spread out. Rulf says they mostly stay near the west end of the Talic Region and are rarely seen by the mountains.

We're chatting about the castle and laughing about a time when Hemot managed to get his foot stuck in a chandelier when Ellcia goes silent. After all we've been through, I immediately go for my sword and spin around, looking for danger. I don't see anything or anyone approaching, and the sky is still clear of Shaloomd.

"I didn't see anything," Ellcia says with a smile.

I calm myself and go back to a normal walk. The others are out of hearing range, at least with the wind blowing in our faces.

"I've just been thinking about something," she says.

"What's on your mind?"

"Just everything that we're learning," she says. "You know, about the Regent, and the rebellion, and about us."

"We don't actually know much at all," I say with a laugh.

"No, but we know some things. Like we know that none of us were born servants. And we know that there seems to be something special about you."

I nod slowly. I'm not sure what I'm supposed to say.

"Rulf looked at you a little funny when he was talking about the Prince."

"I noticed that."

"With that and with what Hob called you and how the Regent centered you out, it makes me wonder something."

I can see she wants to say it, but she's nervous. I decide to dive right in. "Are you wondering if I'm the Prince?"

She's silent for a long time. When she finally speaks, her words come out awkwardly. "No, but that makes a lot more sense than what I was thinking."

"What were you thinking?"

"I thought you might be the son of some really important person, like a nobleman who resisted Regent Parthun's takeover of the kingdom, or maybe the son of a General. But when I think of it, it makes more sense that you might be the Prince."

I feel a little annoyed at her for missing the obvious, but then push that thought aside. "What would you think about that? I mean, if I'm the Prince."

"I'd have to start calling you Your Highness, or Your Majesty, or Prince Roran," she says with a big grin.

"No, I mean, that would certainly change things."

"Well, I've been wondering about how I was called Lady Ellcia by Hob, and how Rulf said that we were all either royalty or children of nobles."

I wait. I'm sure she's about to say something else.

"So," she says, "if you're the Prince, and I'm Lady Ellcia, we could be related."

I feel sick to my stomach again, but I hold it in. "That would be strange."

"Yes. But even if we're not related, and you're Prince Roran, things will change. You'll have to lead the army to take back Sevord City."

"I'm not overly experienced in the whole area of taking back kingdoms or leading armies," I say with a bit of a smile.

"I'm sure someone will help you. Maybe Rulf will just go in and defeat the Regent on his own," she says with a laugh before she grabs my arm. "Let's catch up to everyone else."

We move a little faster until we reach the others. When we catch up to them, Hemot is in the middle of explaining the importance of having a dedicated curtain servant for a castle. "Sure, it seems like I don't do much a lot of the time, but when you have an emergency, you'll be glad to have me."

"Like the time last month when that curtain caught on fire?" I ask, remembering how I put out the fire, and Ellcia and I hung a new curtain.

"Well, yes," Hemot says slowly, "But that's not a good example of how important my position is because I was busy elsewhere."

I give him a look, and he looks away. I remember having found him sleeping behind a suit of armor that day after all the work was done. For good measure, I ask, "Or like the time when we were twelve when all the curtains in the second-floor east-wing corridor were ripped down?"

"Yes!" he says with a big grin.

"… by you," I add.

We all have a good laugh.

By mid-afternoon, we pass through a small village, but we don't stop. Rulf says we have plenty of supplies to make it, and we push on. Just before sunset, we find a forest a little way off the road and settle in for the night.

We hope to reach the foothills by the next day.

15

The Giant

Two days later, we're pushing on through a slow, steady rain. At first, it wasn't too bad. We pulled out the cloaks which Hob had provided for us, and they kept the rain off our shoulders. After a few hours, however, my shoulders felt wet. An hour or so after that, the water ran down my back.

All I want is to be dry again, but the closer we draw to the mountains, the colder it gets. If the sun doesn't come out, we're not going to dry at all.

"You stink even more now!" Marleet hollers.

She's normally the most patient person, especially with Hemot, but I've noticed the wetter she gets, the crankier she gets. I've been giving her a lot of space yesterday and today.

"I can't do anything about that!" Hemot says with a whine in his voice. "I stunk before because I couldn't take a bath. Now I'm in one continual bath, but it's making me stink in a different way!"

Marleet points off to the side of the road. "Well, just walk over there!"

"We're going to have to get used to it," Ellcia pipes in. "I think if we're going to be living in the mining towns, we're not going to have access to comfortable baths like we had in the castle. Those days may be over for a while." She pauses for a moment, and then I hear her quietly whisper, "… maybe forever."

We're all discouraged, and I can't think of any way to pick everyone up. Only Rulf seems unaffected by the rain. He's no more grumpier than usual.

"Ahh!" Mic says. "Rain go away! Rain go away!"

Rulf grunts and takes off his pack. As we walk, he holds it over Mic's head. It doesn't appear to help much, but Mic smiles at Rulf and then waves as if to say that he doesn't need the shelter.

We push on through the endless rain, and by the end of the day, we reach the foothills. At first, it feels like we've entered the mountains themselves, but now and then we catch glimpses of the actual mountains on the far side of the foothills. It's during these times that the sheer size of these formations strikes me in a new way.

With so much cloud cover, it's difficult to know what time of day it is, but we come across a large rock overhang and settle in under it. Once we're all seated and pulling off our cloaks, Rulf heads back out into the rain. I assume he's setting traps.

I would have thought sitting down in a dry place would be much better, but it's not long before we're shivering. Without the movement, the cold creeps in. When Rulf returns, I'm thrilled to see plenty of wood in his arms. It doesn't appear to be too wet, so I assume he found some dry wood under the shelter of other trees or a similar rock overhang. About an hour later, we have a roaring fire, and we've all stripped off as much of our armor and clothing as we feel is appropriate and have set it out to dry.

Rulf disappears again and returns two more times with large armfuls of wood. When he strips off his armor and shirt, I notice two things. First, he smells far worse than all the rest of us combined. Second, his skin is not like ours. I saw his belly in the tavern in Haner, but it was dark. Now that I have more light, I see it looks tough and hangs on his body in some places and is tight in others. Some areas of his belly and chest are gray and covered in strange bumps. He looks far less human without his shirt.

Mic sits down next to him, and I'm reminded yet again of Rulf's cruelty in the midst of his kindness to Mic. The smaller boy's face is still swollen, but it's no longer purple. It's now a darker red. Mic doesn't seem to mind, though. Marleet said she might be able to find a plant that could ease some of the swelling, but Mic literally ran away from her, saying something about not believing in witchcraft.

By the time we're ready for bed, some of our clothing is dry. Hemot, unfortunately, put his shirt too close to the fire, and some of it ended up charred. He seems annoyed with me for that, although I had nothing to do with it. I think we're all still a little upset about the rain.

When I settle for the night, I'm pleased to find that my bedroll is also dry. The nice thing about our packs is that they're mostly waterproof, as long as they're not set down in a puddle or dropped in a river. The material has been well-oiled, and the rain just pours over it and down the sides.

Despite my sore feet and aching legs and joints, I fall asleep quickly. My dreams that night are relaxing and peaceful. I feel like we're finally safe again.

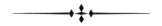

The next morning, I awake once again to Rulf cooking rabbits over the fire. Hemot is already up and appears to have joined Rulf in checking the traps and cleaning the animals.

It's great to wake up to the smell of breakfast in the morning and to feel the warmth of the fire, but what excites me most is that the rain has stopped. The sky's still cloudy, but it looks like it'll be a dry day.

In another hour, all of us are up, we've had our breakfast, and we're back on the road. We still have yet to see another person on the way, aside from those in the village, but that's not surprising. I expect no one travels this road unless they need to.

At about mid-morning, the easterly road brings us to a crossroads. The ways heading north and south, however, are not so much roads as they are paths. Without a word of warning, Rulf turns right and heads south.

"Um," Ellcia calls out from near the back. "Why are we heading that way? Don't we want to continue to the mining village?"

Rulf grunts a reply and keeps walking.

"I'm sorry, Rulf," Ellcia says, her words dripping with sarcasm, "but that's not actually a proper response. Why are we heading south?"

Rulf stops, turns to Ellcia, and grunts again. He looks like he's about to continue on his way when Mic says, "Three peaks. Three peaks."

Rulf grunts yet again. "We don't want that mining village. We want one to the south. There's one at the base of the tri-peak mountain."

He points to the south, and I see what appears to be three peaks off in the distance. It is far enough away that I wish we'd been able to go to Leito and head east from there. As I ponder that, I wonder to myself if that was exactly what

Rulf had intended all along, had the Talic Wolf not taken us off course. I wish the guy would tell us what he's up to.

The walk south takes us between one of the larger foothills and one of the actual mountains. The area, the heights of the mountains, the slopes... everything is stunningly beautiful. The green mountains look almost unreal up close, and the trees and the waterfalls add to the beauty, making the entire display spectacular.

Marleet and Hemot talk as we move along. Marleet has an ability at times to talk non-stop, but Hemot somehow manages to keep up with her. Not only that, but he talks at the same time as her, and both manage to answer each other, ask questions, point out things to one another, and more. It makes my head spin.

Mic is acting a little strange. He's looking around as if he's afraid we're going to be attacked, and he's walking slower than usual. At one point, I ask him if he's alright, but he just laughs and runs on ahead.

At least I have Ellcia. We walk in silence for a while. I see she's bothered about the whole, "Is Caric Prince Roran?" thing, but there's nothing either of us can do about it. We just have to figure it out as we go.

I had never thought of myself as royalty—never thought I was anything beyond a servant. I didn't mind being a servant. Never thought it was a bad thing, but royalty... To be honest... I don't want it.

"I don't know why!" Marleet says a little louder. "Why don't you ask?"

"Why don't you ask?" Hemot says with a laugh.

Marleet replies with another laugh and says, "Why don't YOU ask?"

"STOP IT!" Ellcia hollers. She rarely gets too upset, but Marleet and Hemot have been getting on her nerves. "If you want to ask, ask!"

"Well, now it's no fun," Hemot says, earning him a glare from Ellcia.

"We're wondering if anyone knows why the mountains are green," Marleet asks with a pouty look on her face. "I thought they were green because they were covered in grass or trees or bushes, but it's just greenish dirt."

I roll my eyes, but I don't say anything. I figured it might be something important. The two of them are weird, but they are two of my closest friends. But either way, I'll let Rulf answer this one.

Rulf grunts and moves on.

After a few moments, Mic says, "Use your words. Use your words."

Rulf lets out a growl and explains, "The mountains are full of copper. For some reason, the copper makes the ground turn green."

"Oh," Marleet says. Both she and Hemot look disappointed. I think they were hoping for a more impressive answer.

We move on throughout the day. The path is only wide enough for two people to walk side-by-side for the most part, but now and then the path grows even thinner. I suspect it's rarely used, and even then, people likely walk single file along here. I remember reading about how there used to be thieves in the mountains, but King Hartor had sent half his army to comb through the area. In a matter of weeks, the entire mountain range had been searched and over four hundred thieves had been arrested or killed. The area has been quite safe since.

The thought of King Hartor brings me back to the matter of who I am. Strangely enough, in all my worries that I might be the Prince, I had never considered the fact that being the Prince would mean King Hartor was my dad. If so, that memory of being in the throne room was of the King and me.

A loud roar grabs my attention. All of us drop to the ground without thinking. I feel like at any moment, something huge is going to attack us.

Ahead, the path leads up and over a large hill, and we all move forward carefully. There isn't much room at the top for peering over as the path has become quite thin at this point, but I crawl up there with Rulf and Ellcia.

"What is it?" Hemot whispers up to us.

I stare in shock for a few moments, unable to reply. Neither Ellcia nor Rulf reply either, so I expect it's taken them by surprise as well. On the other side of the hill, down in a valley, sits a large... woman. I try to make sense of what I'm seeing at first because nothing about her seems right. Her head is too large for her body, but then she's not a thin woman. Perhaps it's just the angle. Her clothes are thick and made of patches of every different color, and the style is quite ugly.

Speaking of ugly, the woman is... I catch myself. I don't want to think of people that way. But something is so out of place. I feel like she doesn't fit in with the surrounding landscape.

"Hey!" Hemot hisses again. "What is it?"

"It's a giant," Rulf says.

My eyes bulge as I realize he's right. That's why she doesn't look right. She's quite far from us, but she looks like she's close because of her size. And nothing around her looks right because she's far too big in comparison with everything else. All her proportions are wrong, from her head to her ears to her nose to her arms to her hands to her feet... everything.

I groan as I feel Hemot crawl on top of me to get a better look. Beside me, Ellcia grunts as Marleet comes up on top of her to get a look.

"Wow!" Hemot says as Marleet lets out a gasp.

"Get off me!" I say and push myself back.

We retreat back down the hill, and I ask, "So, do we have to avoid her? Will she attack?"

Rulf grunts, and he looks… uncomfortable. "Don't know. Mic knows more about giants than I do. I didn't like reading about them."

"Giants are dangerous. Giants are dangerous," Mic says.

"Do we need to go around?" Ellcia asks.

Mic doesn't say anything. Instead, he just gives a big, slow nod.

We move carefully over the crest of the hill and leave the path, heading southeast. The giant faces west, and she's not doing much of anything, other than sitting there, so I hope we can manage to get past her without upsetting her. As we descend into the valley, I get a better look. I would guess that she's about twice the height of me, but likely weighs more than all six of us together. She's bulky enough that if she wore clothing that matched the surrounding land, she might be mistaken just for a large boulder. She hasn't moved at all, from what I can tell.

We move through the valley as best we can and reach the other side, making our way carefully. We move up the side of another large hill and finally reach the path just shy of the crest of the hill.

I'm about to think that we'll make it through without being noticed, when Hemot whispers, "Hey Rulf, maybe it's your cousin."

Rulf growls and takes a step toward Hemot, dislodging a few stones on the incline of the path. I turn back to the giant, and my heart feels like it's stopped in my chest. She's finally moved. Her head is turned, and her large black eyes have fixed on us.

"Let's move slowly and carefully up the hill," I say. "Maybe when we're out of sight, she'll forget about us."

We move up the path and reach the top without any more reaction from the giant. I think for a moment that it'll be okay, but just before we're out of sight, the giant lets loose a loud roar and rises to her feet.

We take off down the path, and in a few steps, we're out of sight of the giant. It's big enough, however, that I can hear it stomping up the hill behind us. We run, using the endurance we've built from repeated times of fleeing danger over the last couple of weeks, but a quick glance back tells me we have no chance of getting away.

The giant reaches us and grabs me first. I scream as she pulls me up to her mouth. I don't want the rest to see me so scared, especially Ellcia, but I just can't hold it in. I'm so terrified that I can't even catch a breath. As I get close to her face, she opens her mouth to reveal large square teeth and really bad breath.

The expression on the giant's face changes, and I look down to see all my friends hacking at her legs. It doesn't seem to do much, other than to cut and tear her clothing.

The giant turns her attention back to me and brings me in close to her face. She pushes her nose up to me and smells me like I'm some kind of over-sized flower. When she's done, she drops me to the ground, and I roll away from her, covered in something wet and slimy.

When I come to a stop, Ellcia is in the giant's hand. The other's swords didn't do anything to the giant, but I know mine will. I draw my blade and prepare to kill the giant when Ellcia comes tumbling down near me. I swing the sword out of the way to avoid hurting her and grab her arm. She's covered in the same slimy stuff that's all over me. I've decided that I don't want to think about what it is.

The giant moves through all of us this way, but I notice Rulf has disappeared. I see a slight movement from behind a rock a short distance away. He's hiding. I've never seen Rulf show any kind of fear, but then again, I've never seen him near a giant.

When the giant has finished sniffing my friends, and each of us are covered in a similar disgusting substance, she loses interest in us, but rather than leave, she spins around, looking at all the rocks and bushes. I can't help but think she can smell Rulf. We start to walk on, hoping we're no longer of interest to the massive beast woman. She, however, just runs back and forth. I hate to think of what she'll do if she finds Rulf, but I really don't know what to do about it.

"Move on. Move on," Mic says quietly. "Rulf must hide. Rulf must hide."

"Why does Rulf need to hide?" Marleet asks in a concerned whisper.

Mic shakes his head and says, "Giants don't like giant men. Giants don't like giant men."

Another roar echoes across the hills, and I turn around. The giant has found Rulf, and she has him in her grip. Rulf wrestles hard against her but only manages to wiggle one arm free. She pulls him up to her face and presses her nose against him, smelling him like she smelled us. Unlike us, however, when she finishes smelling him, she bares all her teeth.

Rulf takes his free arm and punches the giant woman directly in her nose. She howls and drops Rulf, who comes barreling after us.

"Run! Run!" Mic says, and we all take off as fast as we can.

"Why doesn't it like me?" Rulf asks in a panic. He's acting strange. Meeting a giant has really thrown him.

"Maybe it just needs to get to know you better?" Hemot offers unhelpfully.

"I don't think that will help," Marleet replies.

Mic laughs at that as we run, but says, "Don't upset Rulf. Don't upset Rulf."

We run on for a few more steps, but the giant catches us with little trouble. We jump out of the way as she seems to have no interest in us, only Rulf.

Everyone draws their swords and attacks, but I stay back. I don't really want to join in, because I know that my sword could end up killing her. But I can't leave Rulf to be eaten—or whatever might happen to him.

The giant grabs Rulf, but he manages to scramble out of her hands. My friends all strike the giant with their swords, and Mic fires a bolt from his crossbow, but everything just bounces off its skin.

The giant has gone from angry to enraged. I don't think she's upset with us at all. She just seems to want Rulf dead! The two battle back and forth. It's obvious Rulf won't win.

I feel regret at what I'm about to do, but I run forward. I launch myself off a larger boulder and managed to get up in the air just enough to plunge my sword, point down, into her back. The blade slides right in as easily as it had through the trees or through anything else I've tried, and the giant roars.

Her arms swing back to try to knock me away, but she can't reach me. I'm horrified when I realize that I'm sliding down her back, not because the sword has released, but because the sword is slicing the giant in two.

I yank back on the sword and tumble onto the ground as the giant falls forward. She screams again, thrashing back and forth for a few more seconds, but then goes quiet.

I shake my head and, even though I'm embarrassed to do it, I break out in tears. I don't know why this one bothered me more than the assassins, but it does. I think with the assassins, I was fighting for my life. This time felt like there might be a choice.

I feel someone pull me to my feet, and arms wrap around me. It takes me a moment to realize it's Rulf.

"Thanks," he whispers. "I know that was hard."

He lets me go but takes my sword from me. After cleaning it on the giant's clothes, he hands it back. I absentmindedly notice that the giant's blood stayed on the sword while the human blood did not. I put the sword in my sheath, and then Marleet grabs my one arm, and Ellcia grabs the other. Together, we walk on, careful not to look behind us.

16

---•---

The Prince

By the end of the next day, we reach the tri-peak mountain. It's too late to move on as it will grow dark soon, so we find what we call a cave, but is more of a deep indent in the side of a cliff. The trees growing on the side of the mountain provide plenty of old, dry wood, and in very little time, we have a roaring fire.

At night, the air around the mountains is cool, so the fire is quite necessary. Rulf says we shouldn't have to worry about any threats here. Giants will stay away from the fire, and there are rarely thieves in the mountains. We settle in to rest our feet and just to chat, when Rulf sits down and says, "Listen up!"

We all stop talking immediately. Rulf hasn't been the most communicative leader, but now and then he tells us something we need to know. We all hope each time is that moment.

"Tomorrow we should reach the mining village. I haven't told you everything."

I smile. I can't wait to hear it all, but then I kind of don't want to hear some of it. I'm scared to find out for sure who I am.

"Are you going to tell us everything now?" Marleet asks.

"No," Rulf says, and we all groan. "But I'll tell you some stuff."

"Captain Tilbur told me I have to protect Caric and get him to the people in the mountain," Rulf explains.

Marleet and Hemot look at me for a moment. Their faces fill with confusion, while Ellcia just stares at the ground. She doesn't look happy. I don't think she wants me to be the Prince.

"Why just Caric?" Marleet asks.

"None of your business," Rulf growls, but then catches himself. "I'm sorry, girl."

"My name is Marleet," she says with a frown.

Rulf stares at her as if he's never seen her before in his life. He points at Hemot. "I thought that one was Marleet. I thought you were Hemot."

"No! I'm Marleet! That's Hemot, and that's Ellcia," she says, pointing at each one in turn.

Rulf gives a confused expression, but I see the sides of his mouth curl up a bit. It's hard to believe, but I think Rulf is trying to be funny again.

"Oh, okay, Marleet. So, tomorrow, we're all going to get to the mining village. We can't let them see our faces. That's important. You have to wear your rain cloaks. Since it's cooler during the day in this area, it might not look strange. Keep your hoods up and your heads down."

"What are we going to do there?" I ask. "If we can't let anyone see us, are we just passing through? If we're here for a while, it'll be hard to keep from being seen forever. Besides, we're going to have to work. The money we have won't last forever."

"We're going into the mine," Rulf explains. "Captain Tilbur wants all of us to go into the mines because the rebels are all there."

We sit in silence for a moment while Rulf watches us. It looks like he's waiting for questions, but I'm not sure what to ask.

Finally, Ellcia asks, "Will the rebels accept us?"

Rulf nods, and Mic answers. "Absolutely. Absolutely."

"How do we get into the mines?" I ask. "I assume only the workers go in there. They might stop us if we try to enter."

"Wagons go into the mines with food and supplies, and then they come out with copper. We'll take one of those wagons. No one will stop us if we're bringing food in for the rebels."

"Won't the owner of whatever wagon we steal complain?" Ellcia asks. "I assume someone will be responsible for the food supply."

Rulf grunts. "We'll have to figure that out. I don't know all the details."

Ellcia leans forward and frowns. "How did the Captain tell you all this in that short little conversation he had with you?"

I think back to when the Captain took Rulf aside. There would be no way for him to share all this with Rulf. Something's not right.

"The Captain and I have been chatting for a long time. I told you he helped me escape the castle, right? Well, he comes out to me all the time and provides food or money to me when I need it."

"Who are you to the Captain that he would do all that?" I ask. I'm trying to see Captain Tilbur as a nice guy, but for my whole life, he's been nothing but cruel.

"I'm the son of one of his closest friends. He and my dad fought together in many wars." Rulf then stands up, grabs his bedroll, throws it down on the ground and crawls in. I gather that means the conversation is over. The rest of us chat for a while. Even Mic joins in now and then, in his own way. Within another hour or so, however, we're all asleep.

Just before noon the next day, we smell smoke.

I'm not worried about a forest fire or anything. There's no sign of that kind of thing, and I assume a forest fire would be hard to miss. I expect we're close to the mining village. A few minutes later, we see children playing in the distance.

I feel nervous. I don't like the idea of having to sneak into the village and steal a cart, but I assume once we find the rebels, they'll return the cart to the villagers. Unless... the villagers and the rebels don't get along.

I'm also nervous about meeting the rebels. From what I've learned in recent days, I'll likely get along better now with the rebels than with the Regent, but I've always thought of the rebels as the bad guys. At least, that's what I was told. I pictured them as mean, grumpy, and dangerous.

We pull our hoods over our heads on a signal from Rulf. With our armor and our hoods up, all of us can easily pass for adults, although Marleet and Ellcia would pass for very thin and somewhat shorter adults.

We reach the crest of a hill. Spread out below us is the village. It's not as large as I had imagined, although I'm reminded that I'm used to living in the largest city in the kingdom. The strange part for me, however, is that the village is spread out much farther than the houses would suggest is necessary.

The village itself is filled with structures made of wood and built on stilts. The stilts are not high—maybe about an arm's length above the ground—but I suspect that's necessary when they have the run-off from the mountains in the spring. I would guess around a hundred buildings are spread throughout the area, all different sizes, and the streets are covered in a thick layer of mud. Horses and oxen pull carts and people walk along, chatting with one another.

On the far side of the village, I see fields of crops. I'm not familiar with farming, but it looks like a lot of food. There's no way this village would need that much. Either they're selling the food in Leito City, or this is one of the primary means of providing for the rebels.

This raises the question in my mind of how many rebels there might be. It had always been suggested that it was a small group of dissidents... but the amount of crops...

To the right, a road leads back toward the Talic Region, disappearing between two smaller hills. On the left, however, is the mountain, and that is where all the action seems to be taking place.

I see four large entrances into the mountain, and all four appear to be in constant use. The two on the far left have carts entering and exiting the mines, while the two on the right appear to be for people. Hundreds of men stream in and out of the caves.

My first thought as I see all the people around the mine entrances is that we'll easily be caught, but then I wonder if the sheer busyness of it all will help to camouflage our movement. We head down into the valley and do our best to act like this is all normal for us.

In the village, I find few people pay any attention to us. Many of the men and women wear hoods, so we don't stand out much. I'm starting to think the rebels don't care who comes and goes through the area, but then I notice a few men watching us. They're not being obvious, but they've positioned themselves against a building here or there, and they seem to always be facing us. At one point, I see one of the men say something to a young child who runs off toward the mountain.

I hope that's not a bad sign.

Rulf leads us deep into the village, and it's not long before my feet are heavy with the sticky mud on the ground. I'm irritated at Rulf for leading us this way as I see the people of the village avoid walking through the main streets. They seem to have found areas closer to the buildings which have less mud. Rulf, however, looks like he enjoys it.

We move toward the mountain and after a half hour or so, we see the staging area for the carts. The wagons sit full of food and supplies, waiting for people to take them in. I watch as three men arrive from the direction of the mountain, grab the reins of the horses hooked up to one of the carts, and lead the cart toward the mines.

We wait about ten minutes, then approach a cart ourselves. No one says anything to us, nor do they pay any attention to us at all, aside from one of the men who watches from a distance. I'm expecting him to sound an alarm, but he says nothing. He just keeps his eyes on us.

Rulf hands the reins of one of the horses to me and takes the other himself. A quick glance back into the cart and I see a mix of food and mining supplies. There are pickaxes and shovels, but also some equipment I don't recognize and some heavy pieces of lumber. I don't know what they could be building inside the caves, but then again, I have no idea what a mine is like.

We pull on the reins, and the horses come without hesitation. In another ten minutes, we've left the village and are well on our way to the mine entrance.

The trail leading toward the mountain is rough. The horses give no trouble, however, which makes me think they do this regularly, back and forth from the village to the mines.

We do our best to steer around the larger of the holes and ditches, but some of them are covered in such thick, muddy water that we don't know how deep they are until a wheel, foot, or hoof goes in. By the time we reach the mines, none of us are happy.

Around the mine entrance sit a dozen or more men. At first, I think they're just lounging about. Many appear to be taking a nap, but as I look around, I see that each one, even the ones who are pretending to sleep, have their eyes on us.

Just before we leave the open landscape and enter the cave, a young boy catches my eye. I know I recognize him from somewhere, but I can't place him. It takes me a few more steps before I remember. He was the young boy in the village—the one the man spoke to.

That boy has alerted the people to our presence.

I hand the reins to Hemot and rush over to Rulf. "Rulf! They know we're here. They're watching us! They're letting us enter the mines!" I feel my heart race as I watch every shadow, expecting a rebel to jump out and attack at any moment.

Rulf just grunts a reply, but Mic says, "We'll be captured. We'll be captured."

I glance back toward the entrance, wondering if we can make a run for it, but ten men stand in the opening. None of them do anything other than watch us. The way back is no longer an option.

Rulf seems nervous but doesn't seem nervous enough to do anything about it. Ellcia looks worried, and Marleet and Hemot seem entirely unaware of any danger. There is, however, no option but to move forward.

The way ahead is cut through rock and dirt. It's wide enough for the cart to easily move along with people walking beside it. Every few steps, large thick boards support the roof of the cave. I now see what some of the pieces of lumber will be used for. There's likely a constant need for more support beams.

I return to the horse I had been leading, but Hemot appears content to carry on. He and Marleet are talking about how they would like to own a horse one day. I make my way over to Ellcia. She doesn't look like she wants to talk. That's fine with me. I just want company.

The floor of the cave is much drier than the ground outside. It's well-worn and solid. The horses don't struggle much in this area.

After about ten minutes, we come across a cave which heads off to the left, moving down into the depths of the mountain. A man sits there at the turn. He's the first one we've seen in the village or mines with a sword. He doesn't appear to be hiding the weapon at all, and something about him gives me the impression that he knows how to use it.

He waves us on as if to say that we can't go down the cave to the left. We don't challenge him. I fear we might have to try to fight our way out of the situation, but I'm so scared. I don't want to hurt anyone, but I also don't want to get hurt.

After the turn, the cave floor slopes upward, and it's not long before we see a group of people ahead. It's difficult to make out details in the dim light of the lamps, but they're clearly waiting for us.

When we reach the men, I'm afraid of a confrontation, but their response confuses me. If they had challenged or threatened us, we would have had to stand our ground. If they had ignored us, we would have just moved on through. Instead, two men simply take the reins of the horses while another two motion for us to follow.

We huddle close together as we move forward. The men don't speak to us at all, although they also don't hide the fact that they're watching us closely. The cart is led down a side cave that descends into the mountain, while we're directed to follow the main cave as it continues at an incline.

We see around thirty soldiers ahead. They stand on each side of the cave, and the men walking with us lead us between them.

Two men from the thirty step away from the soldiers standing on either side of the cave and walk in front of us, while the men who had been walking with us fall away. I look back a few moments later to see the rest of the soldiers following behind. Wherever we're going, there's no going back, and there's no realistic option for fighting our way out.

I find myself next to Mic. All our cloaks are over our faces, but he glances up at me for a moment, and I see his bruised face filled with fear. I don't know what to do, so I put my arm around his shoulders for a moment and give him a side hug. I want to give him confidence, but I fear that my arm is actually shaking with the terror I feel.

Ahead, I see light and hear voices. None of the soldiers have spoken. Unlike the men who had escorted us a few minutes ago, these soldiers only walk ahead and behind. The soldiers in front never look back, and the soldiers behind keep their eyes on us constantly.

We draw closer to the light and voices, and ahead I see a large cavern. We reach it, and I let out a gasp. I hear Ellcia and Marleet give similar reactions, while Hemot whistles. Mic and Rulf don't say anything.

The cavern itself appears to be made of solid stone. I assume it's a natural cave, as the floor, walls, and ceiling are anything but smooth. No support beams run up the sides of the wall in this area, but instead torches line the walls every few feet. It's clearly some kind of meeting space. The ceiling of the cave, which is about three times my height, looks solid, aside from a few places where it runs higher and disappears into the darkness. I see the smoke from the torches move up through those areas.

The soldiers split off as we move into the cave. They head to the left and to the right, taking up position around the perimeter. I glance back to see four soldiers stand sentry in the entrance.

I would guess there's around a hundred people in the cave at the moment. Most are soldiers, but some appear to be nobles, from their attire. In the center of the room stands one man. He's dressed as a soldier, but his armor marks him as a general. I can't quite put my finger on how it is I know this, but he's the one in charge.

"State your business!" the man bellows. His voice echoes through the cavern and carries such authority that I feel like I want to run and hide behind the others.

Rulf whispers to us, "Keep your hoods up." He steps forward and hollers, although with nowhere near the authority the general offered, "Who are you, and where do your loyalties lie?"

Many of the soldiers reach for their swords at Rulf's reply, but the General motions for them to stand down. My heart races so fast and loud that I'm afraid I'll miss what the General says. I try to control my heart, but between the fear that we'll be killed and the fear that I might be the Prince, there's no hope of calm.

"I am General Lirnal of the Armies of Sevord, loyal subject to the Royal Line. My loyalties are to Prince Roran and to the throne, and I stand against the usurper, Regent Parthun." He steps forward and places a hand on the hilt of his sword and hollers loud enough that I nearly stumble back, "Now, state your business!"

Instead of answering, Rulf pulls back his hood. I don't know if the rest of us are supposed to follow his example, but the others don't move, so I keep my hood up as well.

The General steps forward a little more and stares at Rulf's face for a moment before he smiles. "There is no doubt about it. You must be Rulfor. I'd recognize you anywhere. You look just like your father!" His smile grows even larger. "When the castle fell, we thought you had been killed."

Rulf gives a simple, but respectful, bow. "No, General. I survived. I couldn't find my parents, and Captain Tilbur sent me out of the castle to protect me."

The General smiles and said, "Well, Rulfor, I'll have no trouble finding your parents." He waves to a soldier and orders, "Go find them. I think Traltor is terrorizing the cooks, and Nareesa is probably with him."

A soldier runs off, and Rulf asks in disbelief, "My parents are alive?"

The General nods and says, "They are. If we had known you were alive, your dad would have torn down Sevord brick by brick to find you. Tilbur could only send brief messages in code out to us. There have been no real details. We knew someone was coming, but we had no idea who or when you would get here. But, tell me, who are these people?"

Rulf stands straight, and from my position, I can make out a broad smile. I'm not sure if it's because he just learned about his parents or if it's because of his announcement. In a loud voice, he announces, "I have brought the Prince of Sevord with me: Prince Roran."

My heart races. I'm absolutely terrified. I didn't want it to go like this. If I'm really the Prince, I don't want to have to step forward. I want someone else to push me forward. As if she were reading my mind, Ellcia gives me a shove.

I stumble forward, and all eyes turn to me. All I can think of is that I want to be back in the castle, cleaning some statue. When I was there, I didn't know what was really going on, but at least it was easy.

This is not.

I pull back my hood, and General Lirnal gasps. I see his eyes fill with tears, and he moves toward me. He grabs each of my shoulders and with a shake in his voice, he exclaims, "Tilbur kept you alive!" The General wraps his arms around me and squeezes me tight.

I can't help but think this is not the way a General approaches a Prince. I ask, "Tilbur?"

"Yes," the General says. "Captain Tilbur… your uncle. I had suspected you might have survived, and I hoped Tilbur would be able to care for you. Tilbur is my brother. We are… you're my nephew."

My mind races through that, and I realize that it makes sense. I knew Tilbur was technically a prince and in line for the throne, but far enough down that he would never be king.

The General steps back suddenly, and says, "But our reunion must wait. The son of my oldest brother, King Hartor is here. Prince Roran, I beg of you, step forward."

That I didn't expect. So… I'm not the prince… but… who is?

I turn in shock and stare at Hemot. He pulls back his hood, and the look on his face is one of confusion. I hear someone quietly say, "He looks like the Milterite…" but aside from that, there's no other reaction. I'm so confused. I want to shake my head and cry.

I hear a thud, and Mic's armor drops to the ground. I feel relief suddenly as he comes back into focus after so long of wearing the enchanted armor. He steps forward, throws back his hood, and announces in a clear voice, "I am Prince Roran."

The General steps forward for a moment to stare at Mic's face, and then falls to his knees along with everyone else. I hear one of the nobles say in a choked voice, "It's really him," and another says, "He looks just like his father."

The look on the General's face then fills with rage. He stands up and demands, "Who struck you?"

"I did, General," Rulf says.

The swords of every soldier in the room, including the General, come out. I see even the nobles have knives in their hands. I'm about to run to Rulf's side when Mic runs in front of Rulf. "General, no! He was following my orders. I ordered him to strike me to help disguise me. Please, I beg you. Do not harm him."

The General turns back to Mic, or Prince Roran, and says with tears in his eyes, "My Prince, you never have to beg me. I am your servant. I will obey every word. I will not harm him."

A loud crash sounds out from the other side of the cave as three armor clad soldiers roll to the side. What appears to be a giant comes barreling through a smaller cave, dwarfing everyone around. Coming up beside him is a small woman—no, she's not small. She's taller than all the men, but she's tiny compared to the giant of a man who's entered the room.

Without thinking, I pull out my sword. My weapon was the only one that could kill a giant the last time, and I fear it will be the same this time.

I pause, however, as the man hollers out, "Rulfor? Where are you, my boy?"

The woman at his side zeros in on Rulf. She gasps and points. "That's him! He's alive."

Both charge forward, and I feel myself yanked back out of the way as soldiers grab me. Ellcia, Hemot, and Marleet are also dragged out of the way, and the General and four soldiers take up position in front of Mic. I realize, however, that no one is trying to stop the giant. They're just trying to keep out of his way to minimize the damage.

"Ma? Pa?" Rulf says in a very childish voice. I find my eyes filling with tears as I watch the reunion. Rulf appears beside himself with joy, and I can see the resemblance between him and his father—although his father is significantly larger.

"Ma! Pa!" Rulf says again. "I protected Prince Roran all these years. I brought him back to you."

"WHERE IS HE?" Rulf's father bellows. When his eyes land on Mic, he rushes forward.

General Lirnal cries out, "No, Traltor, wait…" but Rulf's father knocks him and the other soldiers aside. When he gets to Mic, he grabs Mic's hand roughly and kisses Mic on the back of the hand.

Mic looks with disgust at his hand dripping with… grossness… but then Rulf's mom lifts Mic right off the ground in an embrace. She then kisses Mic all over his face. I see him struggle, but no one intervenes. I get the impression that Traltor and Nareesa's ways are tolerated. Or no one can stop them.

"Traltor, Nareesa," General Lirnal hollers. "I know you are excited to have Prince Roran back, but you have to treat him with respect. Remember, he is our future king."

Nareesa drops Mic to the ground and turns to the General. "But I used to change his diapers," earning an uncomfortable look from Mic.

"And I used to give him his nightly baths," Traltor says, earning a confused look from everyone.

"You were my… nannies?" Mic asks.

"No!" Nareesa says with a laugh. "We were just good friends with your ma and pa! And we wanted some experience with kids before little Rulfor here was born."

"You will call them the King and Queen!" General Lirnal orders. "At some point, you two are going to have to realize that it is improper to speak of royalty in such a manner."

Traltor laughs, shakes his head, and reaches over to ruffle General Lirnal's hair. "Of course, Lirnal," Traltor says.

"We'll be respectful." Traltor and Nareesa then return to Rulf and, without another word, lead him away.

A few of the Nobles around the room approach Mic. They bow to him and then speak with him. I turn back to my friends to see big smiles on Hemot and Marleet's faces and a look of relief on Ellcia's face.

She comes in close and gives me a hug. She holds on for a long time, and I hear her whisper, "I think I like this better than you being the Prince."

"Me too," I whisper back.

The General clears his throat, and we all turn to face him. "Well, we have a lot to figure out. I suspect some of you might have family or close friends of your family here. Most of the nobility fled when Parthun killed my brother, the King, along with many of the king's loyal subjects."

I turn to Mic who seems unsure of himself. I'm not surprised by that. I would hate to be in his position right now. I suddenly realize that I don't actually know Mic. Everything I thought about him was wrong. I feel like I've never actually met him before.

"Now what?" Marleet asks. "I mean, now that the Prince has been found… what do we do?"

The General puts a hand on my shoulder and then says to Marleet and the rest of us. "Now?" Before continuing, he lets out a loud laugh. "Now it's time to return Prince Roran to his throne, remove the usurper, and crown Roran the new King of Sevord!"

Continued in The Lost Kingdom
Book Two of the Sevordine Chronicles.

Pronunciation Guide

Now, you might think that I have tried to create a proper pronunciation guide, but I don't know how to do that. I could look it up, but not only do I not understand diacritical markings, but I think most people don't. So… I made a pronunciation guide that makes sense to me with the capital letters pointing out the emphasis.
And here it is.

Berin	BARE-rinn
Caric	CARE-ick
Corter	CORE-ter
Draydon	DRAY-dunn
Ellcia	ell-CEE-ah
Farnum	FAR-num
Frindor	FRIN-door
Frippolee	FRIPP-oh-lee
Granel	GRA-nell
Gratter	GRA-terr
Haner	HAY-ner
Hartor	HAR-terr
Hella	HELL-ah
Hemot	HEM-mot
Hillbin	HILL-binn
Leito	LAY-toh
Lirnal	LIR-nall
Marleet	mar-LEET
Morgin	MOR-ginn
Nordin	NOR-dinn
Parthun	PAR-thunn

Rainer	RAY-nerr
Reber	REE-berr
Relin	RELL-linn
Shaloomd	sha-LOOM-d
Shalsee	SHALL-see
Shawn	AWE-some
Talic	TAL-ick
Tallia	TAL-lee-ah
Tilbur	TILL-burr
Trevolay	TREV-oh-lay

CHECK OUT THESE BOOKS BY
Shawn P. B. Robinson

Adult Fiction (Sci-fi & Fantasy)

The Ridge Series (3 books)
ADA: An Anthology of Short Stories

YA Fiction (Fantasy)

The Sevordine Chronicles (5 Books)

Books for Younger Readers

Annalynn the Canadian Spy Series (6 Books)
Jerry the Squirrel (4 Books)
Arestana Series (3 Books)
Activity Books (2 Books)

www.shawnpbrobinson.com/books

Printed in Great Britain
by Amazon

34492792R00121